MAX'S CAMPERVAN CASE FILE 6

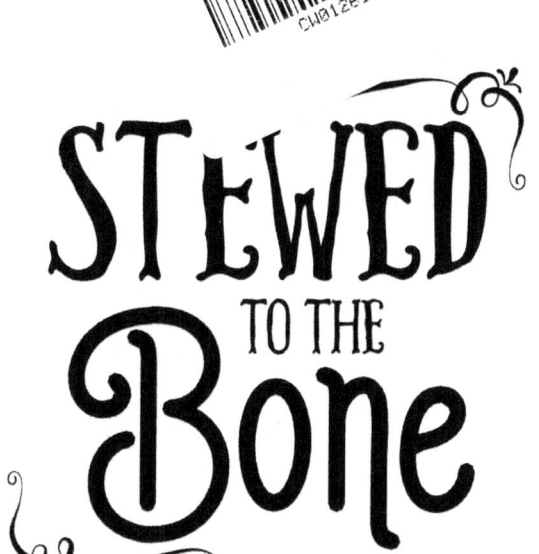

STEWED TO THE Bone

TYLER RHODES

Copyright © 2024 Tyler Rhodes

All rights reserved. This book or any portion thereof may not be reproduced or used in any manner whatsoever without the express written permission of the author except for the use of brief quotations in a book review.

This is a work of fiction. Names, characters, businesses, places, events and incidents are either the products of the author's imagination or used in a fictitious manner. Any resemblance to actual persons, living or dead, or actual events is purely coincidental.

Dedicated to everyone who puts their tent up in the garden to dry out properly after a camping trip. No mould for you!

Chapter 1

"Cooee!" Mum waved excitedly from the far side of the field, her high-pitched, eager call causing the entire campsite to stop what they were doing and check out the surprising visitor to our small slice of paradise.

I waved back, happy to see her, and heaved from my chair. The grass felt nice and cool on my bare feet on this glorious, warm morning as I hurried to greet her.

Anxious slid out from under my 67 VW campervan, his favourite spot as he loved Vee, our home on wheels, and the cool shade it afforded him. Tail already spinning faster than a jet's engines, he barked happily as he tore across the field towards "Grandma."

"Max, it's me," called Mum utterly unnecessarily, as who else could it be?

As usual, she was dressed immaculately, although it was utterly impractical for camping. Mum and Dad were fifties fanatics, and stuck to the fashion of the era. With her make-up flawless, her lips ruby red to match not only the bandanna holding back startlingly bright red hair but also her dangerously high heels, she stood in the middle of the field and twirled. Mum's trademark polka dot dress flared out and sparkled as it caught the sun. I half expected her to click her heels together and declare, "We're not in Kansas anymore."

"Hi, Mum," I called, waving again and smiling. Shaking my head as she made her way gingerly towards us, I marvelled at her dedication to fifties fashion and downright refusal to wear appropriate footwear.

Anxious knew better than to launch at Mum, a fan of mud on her outfits she was not, so skidded to a halt and sat beside her, eyes locked on the giver of plentiful treats, body trembling in anticipation as he barked a greeting.

"He's been desperate to see you ever since I told him this morning that you and Dad were coming. Um, where is he?"

"He's such a good boy," laughed Mum, her carefree, positive outlook on life something I always admired.

"Dad's a good boy?"

"No, Anxious." Mum frowned at the confusion, then smiled as she bent to make a fuss of probably the cutest Jack Russell Terrier in existence. And he knew it.

As Mum stroked his white and brown fur, and Anxious sighed, I moved in for a hug and we embraced. She always smelled of strong perfume and all the hair products ever invented, but it was familiar, comforting, and at least you knew where you stood with her. Never with a lit match too close, that was for sure.

"I can't wait for our holiday." We broke apart then locked arms so I could help her over to my pitch.

"I'm surprised you said yes. When I suggested you both come and have a few days camping with us, I assumed you'd say no. You barely made it through the night when you stayed in the campervan. You're more a posh hotel and swimming pool kind of person."

"Don't be daft!" Mum scolded, but with a smile as she batted at my beard like it was about to attack her.

"Hey, what was that for?"

"You remind me of a Yeti. That big beard, and the long hair. It's got lighter from the sun, so now you're like a bear that's been on holiday."

"Do bears go on holiday?" I teased, my mood already lifted as we fell into the usual banter.

"Of course they do, you stupid boy. How else would they relax?"

"I honestly have no idea," I admitted.

"And stop changing the subject. Why are you so scruffy? Those cut-off jeans are frayed, and your vest is too little. Have you been working out? Your muscles look big. But you've caught too much sun. You look muddy. Your blue eyes are almost green now. That always used to happen when you were a lad if you got a deep tan in the summer. Why are you smiling?" Mum stood on tiptoe to peer into my eyes. Her short stature in no way meant she couldn't stare down anyone, even if I was six one and she hardly came up to my chest.

"I'm just happy to see you and get told off even though I'm a man in his thirties," I laughed. "But what made you decide to come and stay here in the middle of nowhere? I know I asked, but what's the reason?"

"Because we missed you, of course. And your father, if he ever bothers to move our lovely new home, promised I could choose what we stayed in. Oh, it's awesome," beamed Mum. "You wait until you see it."

"Any problems finding the place?" I asked, trying to keep a straight face. Neither were the best with directions, both mistrusting sat nav or Google Maps, preferring old-fashioned maps Mum had a habit of reading upside down or using the wrong page, much to Dad's frustration.

"None at all," she mumbled.

"You sure?"

"Of course. We may have taken a teensy detour, but it was nice and scenic and I fancied the drive."

A car beeped so we both spun to the open gate. I glanced from Mum back to the bizarre scene and shook my head.

"Dad, I assume?" My eyebrows threatened to launch from the top of my head as I gawped at the peculiar sight.

"Isn't it divine?" squealed Mum, dumping her bag and the caravan keys on the picnic bench then waving both her arms and doing a little jig. "We picked it up a few hours ago, but your father is having issues. I told him I'd drive, but he insisted I'd crash, so I left him to play. I said I'd get the gate, but would you mind? These heels keep getting stuck in the floor."

"Mum, it's not a floor. It's the ground. Earth and grass. You need to change into your trainers. You did bring them, didn't you? And your walking boots?"

"Of course I did, but we aren't walking yet."

"You just walked," I insisted. "But yes, I'll get the gate."

Anxious remained by Mum's side while I hurried over to Dad, trying not to grin too much but failing miserably.

"Do not," warned my stressed-out father with a scowl, "say a word."

"Wasn't going to," I replied, deadpan. "You okay reversing with that, er, caravan?" I hid my smile with my hand, but my sides were hurting and I knew I couldn't hold back my laugh for long.

"Don't you dare laugh! I had to drive this stupid thing for miles. And now I've got to reverse across the field. Which way do you turn the steering wheel to get it to go in a straight line? It's impossible. Took me ages to get through the gate."

"You'll figure it out," I said happily, then reached through the open car window and hugged my disgruntled, red-faced, very sweaty father. His hair, normally slicked back with Brylcreem in his usual fifties style, was rather dishevelled, his white T-shirt with rolled sleeves to showcase his trim figure was bunched up, and his Levi's 501s with fat turn-ups were hidden beneath the map he'd clearly taken off Mum to try to read.

"Help me out here, Son," said Dad in a panic as he glanced in the side mirror. "Your mother's been a nightmare with this thing. I'm desperate to get it parked and never look at it again."

"Good luck with that. What possessed you to get it?"

"I had no choice. She insisted. It was this, or we wouldn't come. Anything for a quiet life. And I wanted to see you. Catch up on your adventures."

"Okay, so you just have to remember that everything is the opposite when reversing. If the caravan starts going right, you have to turn left. And vice-versa." I nodded, then headed towards the gate.

"Wait!" Dad called. "The right in the mirror, or if I was staring at it from here? Or from behind?"

"The right in the mirror," I called back, having absolutely no idea how to reverse with a caravan or what the rules were. The one time I'd tried reversing with a small trailer, I'd got so exasperated I just unhitched it and pulled it into our drive.

With the gate closed, I ambled across the campsite, waving at the people I'd come to know a little. It was a small, intimate place with spots for tents or small campervans but no electric hook-up. Nestled in amongst trees and hedges, most pitches were very private, with a small fire box and a picnic bench at no extra cost.

It had been a relaxing, quiet, and enjoyable few days. The perfect antidote to events a few weeks ago when a fun music festival had become one filled with fear and an intriguing double murder mystery I finally helped solve with Min, my ex-wife and best friend besides Anxious. It was a shame she couldn't join us here, but she had work and I had my life as a nomad. Plus, and it pained me to even think about it, we were no longer together.

I was doing my best to ensure that changed, but we'd agreed to wait a year before considering our future. At least, I'd agreed. She'd insisted. It was fair enough after the mess I'd made of everything, but my new vanlife had been perfect for me, and I had finally found my true calling. Helping out the communities I encountered, and solving a seemingly endless number of murder mysteries.

Anxious barked directions along with Mum, causing quite a stir at the sleepy campsite. With little else to do on this scorching Friday morning, everyone was partaking in the best form of entertainment available and watching the noobs make a right mess of arriving.

Dad was reversing, but the bright pink, bubble-like caravan larger than any I'd ever seen before was almost at a right angle to the car. He pulled forward, then tried again, but this time it jackknifed the other way. I waved at him through the window as he straightened up again, but he scowled and wiped his face with his arm, sweat pouring into his eyes.

"Need a hand?" I offered innocently.

"No chance. I've made it this far and I will not let this pink monstrosity get the better of me," he snapped.

"Suit yourself." Whistling, I sauntered over to Mum.

She called out instructions like, "Left a bit. No, the other left. On my side," or, "Now do that but in a straight line," which was definitely helping no end.

"It's very pink," I noted.

"Isn't it?" she gasped, smiling happily, oblivious to her husband's rising stress levels. "And apparently it's got lots of room, a proper toilet, and even a shower. And a nice kitchen."

"You didn't look inside?"

"We were running late, and I wanted it to be a nice surprise for when we were together. Apparently, the interior is pink too. It's their special caravan."

"Special?"

"Yes, you know, for people who want some class."

I checked on Mum, but she was being serious, so nodded my agreement then jumped as Dad beeped the horn, the hazard lights blinked on, and he stalled the car.

Ten minutes later, Dad emerged from the car looking like a sweaty beetroot and stomped over to us. "There's something wrong with it. The wheels must be wonky. It won't reverse."

"That's your rubbish driving," said Mum helpfully.

"My driving is fine," he huffed. "It's that pink eyesore that's rubbish. Maybe the axle's bent or something?" He shrugged. "It's fine there anyway."

"You can't leave it there! It's not in the right place. You need to reverse it so it's next to Max's campervan. His is straight and even up on ramps so it's level. Have we got ramps?"

"No, we don't," grumbled Dad.

"It's nice and flat if you can get it there," I said, pointing to the level ground beside Vee the other side of the picnic bench.

"I told you, it's not working. We got a duff caravan."

"Let me have a go," declared Mum, then, miracle of miracles, she slipped off her high heels and marched towards the car.

"This will be entertaining." The man I looked up to most in the world winked as he crossed his arms, preparing for the show.

Ten seconds later, Mum hopped out of the car, slapped her hands together, nodded to us, then asked, "Is the kettle on?"

We gawped at her then the perfectly parked caravan lined up with millimetre precision in the allocated spot.

"How did you do that?" asked Dad.

"Easy. You just have to turn right if you want it to go left."

"See, I told you," I said, smugness radiating.

"You both made me do it wrong with your confusing instructions!" Dad smiled and laughed, never one to stay grumpy for long.

He pulled me into a hug then stepped back, looked

me up and down, and grunted.

"What?"

"You look good. Strong, tanned, and very hairy. You've got my genes."

"I wish he did," sighed Mum. "His are frayed and he's cut them off."

"I meant he takes after me. A full head of hair and very handsome."

"Thanks. So, fancy a cuppa?"

"Too right. I'm parched. Why is it so hot?"

"Because you were stressed doing your silly parking," said Mum. "And it's the middle of summer. This is a lovely place, Max. How did you find it?"

"I did some research before I left the music festival. We're heading down to Devon and Cornwall, and this looked like a great place to visit. Nice and quiet. I know we're not too far south, so figured you might enjoy a break. Although, Uncle Ernie was miffed you didn't come and see him at Lydstock."

"I spoke to him about that. You know it isn't our thing. But well done for solving the murders. That sounded wild." Dad's eyes widened, keen to get the full story.

"It was. But Ernie was a real star. Maybe next year?"

"Maybe."

"I hope you do go. He'd appreciate it."

Anxious vanished, then came trotting out from Vee with his lead in his mouth.

"As subtle as always," Dad sniggered. "Fine, we'll go for a walk, but not a long one."

"Don't say the W word!" Mum and I shouted, but it was too late.

Anxious dropped the lead and ran around us, barking his head off, before grabbing it again and whipping around so it smacked Dad in the shins, then repeated the game until I managed to snatch the lead.

"He can run free around here, and the woods are

cool, so let's take him for a stroll then have a cuppa," I suggested.

Twenty minutes later, he'd run himself ragged because he was so excited, so we returned to the campsite and hurried under the sun shelter.

The kettle whistled, so while Anxious recovered I made the tea, arranged the camping chairs under the sun shelter, and we settled down.

"You're getting good at setting things up." Mum sipped her tea and studied my setup. "You've got your outdoor kitchen very neat, with everything in those plastic boxes, and Vee is gleaming."

"Thanks. I'm getting into the swing of this properly now. I always sort out the kitchen first under the sun shelter, stack everything, and I gave the campervan a thorough clean yesterday."

"Don't you miss a proper home?" asked Dad. "Your own bed, somewhere to watch the TV? What about a bathroom? That's so much hassle. And no bath." Dad shuddered. He loved soaking for hours at a time.

"It's definitely a lot to get used to," I admitted. "Sometimes I crave those things, but mostly not. I feel more connected living a simpler life. Like I'm part of the world, not a bystander. Yes, there are some things that take longer and are more trouble, but I'm out of the rat race thanks to the property investments from when I was a chef, and am the happiest I've ever been."

"That's not quite true, is it?" he asked.

"Maybe not."

"You were happiest with Min. Before you ruined it by working ungodly hours and neglecting her. She divorced you because you were obsessed with work and being a top chef rather than a top husband."

"Blimey, no need for that. I know what I did, but I'm a new man. As soon as she divorced me, I realised what an idiot I'd been and changed my life. Our year apart made me realise a lot about myself, so I packed it all in. So, yes, this is the right decision and I adore vanlife."

"It's your true calling," agreed Dad. "So, when are you and Min getting back together? We miss her."

"We do," agreed Mum.

"You both know the deal. She wants a year to find herself. It's a lot for her to handle, and we might be best friends now, but our first year divorced was us mostly just reeling from the impact, sorting out the finances, and getting ourselves right in the head. She's still unsure what to do. I know what I want, but we'll see. All I can do is try my best."

"She should have come to stay with us here," said Mum.

"She's got her own life. It's better if she isn't around too often."

"Why?"

"Because she doesn't want to give me false hope or confuse herself. You don't jump back into a relationship after what we went through unless you know it's for life. She needs to know I won't ever act that way again."

"She's way too good for you," said Dad, smiling.

"She sure is," I chuckled.

We chatted more while we drank our tea, but in the end I had to say what Dad and I were both thinking. "I need to move. I can't sit and stare at that thing a moment longer."

"Me either. It's hurting my eyes."

"It's adorable," said Mum.

We studied the pink caravan. Dad and I shuddered, Mum smiled happily, Anxious sat with his back to it.

"Let's have a look inside," insisted Mum.

"Why don't you do the honours?" Dad asked me.

"Me? Why? Let Mum go in first."

"No, you do it," she said. "Describe it to me. It'll be fun."

"Okay, if you insist."

I took the keys from the picnic bench, unlocked the little door, opened it wide and secured the latch, then pulled down the steps and went inside.

"Well, what do you see?" asked Mum.

Gasping, and feeling queasy, I jumped out, shook from head to toe as nausea rose, and said, "I see a body on the floor. He's as pink as the interior. He's naked, and he, er, he looks cooked."

"Cooked?" asked Dad.

"Yes, cooked. Like he's been stewed. Stewed to the bone!"

Chapter 2

"Very funny," sighed Dad, shaking his head. "You had me going for a moment. I know you've dealt with some gruesome things lately, but you shouldn't wind us up like that. Your poor mum's gone green."

"I am not green. But I do feel a bit funny." Mum staggered forward and leaned against the caravan, then straightened out, smiled, and said, "You naughty boy."

"I'm not joking. Seriously, there's a man in there. A naked man. He's almost as pink as this monstrosity of a caravan. I know cooked meat when I see it. Someone's boiled him or slow-roasted."

"Can you see his todger?" asked Mum, eyebrows raised.

"What? Yes, of course. He's naked," I said, confused.

"I'm not having that!" She brushed past me and thundered up the steps into the caravan.

"We need to get her out," I told Dad, then jumped inside to stop Mum from seeing such a ghastly sight.

Dad followed right behind, grumbling about this being a poor joke, but he soon ate his words as we found Mum leaning against the counter of the compact kitchenette, staring at the corpse.

"You weren't messing around, were you?" said Dad.

"Of course not. Mum, come outside. You don't need to see this."

Her eyes tracked up to me, face ashen, then to the caravan's interior. Dad and I took a moment to study the furnishings, too, and it made me almost as nauseous as the body at our feet.

"It's very pink, isn't it?" Mum grinned as she took in the small table with bench seats covered in pink velour, then the walls of pale pink, the kitchen tiles, no guesses as to colour, and through an open door I spied a bed taking up the entire tiny room with, of course, very frilly covers matching the walls.

"It's utterly ghastly," groaned Dad. "How are we meant to sleep in here? I'll have nightmares."

I turned to him, so close I could see the hairs in his ears, and asked, "You don't think the smell, or the fact a cooked naked dude was in here will put you off more?"

"Of course it will! But there's just so much pink."

"I think it's divine. Very tasteful," gasped Mum as she ran a hand along the pink fake quartz counter then locked eyes on the kettle. "Ooh, how sweet. It matches everything else, and is in it's own little metal cage so it doesn't rattle around. I knew this was a great caravan."

My mouth opened and closed, but no words would emerge. My parents never failed to amaze me. Strong-willed, set in their ways, yet adventurous and full of the joy of life, they took whatever happened to them in their stride and had always been very supportive. What they weren't was tactful. Both missed the day it was handed out and took an extra dose of oblivious, then loaded up on unfounded self-confidence.

"I think we better get out of here," I insisted. "We're contaminating a crime scene and it's not fair on whoever this is to be talking about kettles in front of him."

"He won't mind," said Mum cheerily. "He's dead. Ooh, ooh, do we get to solve the mystery with you, Max? We're actually here right at the start, so we can help. I'll be your sidekick, and Jack can make the teas and chase after us as we hunt for clues and close in on the murderer."

"Why do I have to make the teas?"

"Because I'm the sidekick. Tell him, Max. He's rubbish at this already, isn't he?" Mum poked Dad in his belly, still firm with his tight T-shirt tucked into his jeans.

"I am not! I helped figure things out back on Max's first adventure. Tell her, Max."

"Let's just get outside," I sighed, forgetting what they were like once they got an idea in their heads. "And don't touch anything."

"Oops," said Mum as she dropped a pink tea towel over the man's head.

"Mum!"

"He was staring at me. It was putting me off."

I ushered them out, then paused to study the body properly. The man must have been in his forties, with a definite dad bod. Not fat, but he clearly never exercised or worried about what he ate. His hair was light brown, a scruffy cut with a slight curl, and he had two earrings in his left ear. I could picture his face perfectly, even though Mum had covered his head with the tea towel. There was no wedding ring, no tattoos, or anything to identify him beyond appearance. What I found most interesting was that he truly was cooked.

Who does that? How do you do that? You'd need a massive pot, that was for sure. There was no sign of anything having been disturbed. In fact, the caravan was immaculate, and had clearly been cleaned thoroughly after it was last used. So why was the man inside? How had he got here? And for what possible reason?

Questions raced past, one after the other, and I knew without doubt that I was up to my neck in another murder mystery of very gruesome proportions.

And yet the chef side of me couldn't help but wonder about the process. As disgusting as it was, it was an admittedly impressive feat. I tried not to focus on the details of the body before me in such a morbid way, but a tiny part of me still marvelled at how this was accomplished.

The smell became too much, so I moved to leave, almost tripping over Anxious as he sat waiting patiently, eyes fixed on the corpse. His nose twitched as he took in the smell, but he knew something wasn't right and this was taboo meat, most definitely off the menu.

"It's a nasty one, isn't it?" I asked, knowing he was a sensitive soul.

Anxious' eyes met mine, he let out a whine, wagged his tail once, then stood and skipped outside, barking for me to follow.

I took several deep breaths, then closed the door and moved over to the sun shelter where my guests were busy quarrelling in the loving way they always had and I knew always would. The familiarity of their relationship, their love for each other and for me, was a comfort, and I gave thanks for having them in my life.

To an outsider it might seem like they argued a lot, but it was always with a light-hearted side. Just their way. They'd never had a true fight in their entire long relationship, and I'd enjoyed a happy home life and could always count on them. Even if they were utterly bonkers.

"Cup of tea?" asked Mum as she shoved a mug into our hands, beaming. "Look at my boys all geared up to solve the crime of the century."

"Um, thanks for the tea. Aren't you freaked out? He's cooked in there. In your caravan."

"I'm sure it'll clean up with a squirt of bleach. I'll go get it."

"No, you can't go sloshing bleach around in there! And why did you bring it?"

"Oh, yes, of course. It might ruin the cushions. And always come prepared, that's my motto."

"Your motto is, 'Do what I say or I'll glare,'" countered Dad.

"Is not!" Mum glared at him until he wilted.

After a deep breath, I explained, "I'm not worried about the cushions. I'm worried about you destroying evidence. Bleach will get rid of things the forensics team might uncover. No cleaning."

"Not even a quick sweep? I don't want the police to think I don't run a tight ship."

"Love, the caravan was obviously cleaned before we got it," explained Dad. "Max is right. You can't go interfering."

"Interfering? Me?" she asked, aghast, adjusting her bandanna. "When have I ever interfered in my life?" Dad and I exchanged a knowing look, but neither of us said anything. "I saw that. You two better not be conspiring."

"We weren't conspiring," Dad mumbled.

"Good. Now, drink your tea."

It was actually a nice cuppa, and I did need it, so sipped it slowly and tried to think.

"He's got that look," Dad told Mum.

"He has," she agreed.

Anxious barked his agreement, tail swishing, unable to decide which of us to look at, so he ducked under Vee and watched all three instead.

"What look have I got?"

"Excited, pensive, thoughtful, and confused," said Dad.

"You know me too well," I laughed. "Guys, I'm pleased you're here, but we need to think this through. Let's start at the beginning. Who did you get the caravan off?"

"Some place a few miles away. Right weird set-up it was," said Dad, warming to things now he was the focus. "They had this massive lot full of caravans and campers. Hundreds of them. They sell them, store them, even hire out stupid-looking ones for hen do's and stag parties. That's what ours is. A party caravan for women to get drunk in and have male strippers parading around in their Y-fronts."

"I don't think male strippers wear Y-fronts," I told him.

"You mean they go commando?" gasped Dad, glaring at Mum.

"I haven't had any strippers in there. Especially without their undies on."

"You better not," he warned.

"And it's not a party caravan," insisted Mum. "It's just a nice colour. It's fun."

"Mum, it looks exactly like the kind of thing women on a hen do would rent for a weekend at a campsite. But that's beside the point. How did you hear about the place? Why there?"

"I called up the campsite to check on things. I know you booked it for us, but I wanted to be sure. I asked the nice lady about renting a caravan so we didn't have to tow it far, and she said her son worked at a rental place just up the road. It's called Sunny Parks. She even sent me the photos of the pink one as I said I wanted something tasteful and not too masculine, so she arranged to book it for me."

"And I paid for it," snapped Dad. "Cost a fortune."

"Stop interrupting! As I was saying, she arranged it and we collected it earlier. The son was quite keen, and fawning over me. I think he fancied me."

"He was in his twenties!"

"And?" asked Mum, giving Dad "that look" which meant tread carefully if you want any dinner.

"Nothing," he mumbled.

"So then we paid, and we came here."

"But you weren't shown inside?"

"No. Like I said earlier, I wanted it to be a surprise. And the lad was busy, and seemed pre-occupied, so we signed the forms and left. That's okay, isn't it?"

"Yes, of course. Just trying to get things straight. And where was the caravan when you arrived?"

"It was around the side of the building. Not with the

others. It was by a loading bay thing. Not sure why."

"I do," said Dad smugly. "It was because it's ugly and bright pink. They didn't want anyone else to see it."

"Don't be stupid."

"Okay, that makes sense. So, either at Sunny Parks or while we were out walking Anxious, someone put the body in there. It can't have been in there too long as it would be, er, more smelly otherwise. Maybe they have CCTV. Either that, or someone came here and dropped the body off. That's unlikely as there are people here, so maybe it wasn't even meant to be rented out and the body was being hidden."

"He's so good at this," gushed Mum, beaming at me.

"That's my lad," agreed Dad, pride in his eyes.

"I'm just letting my mind wander. Thinking about it. But we do need to call the police now. I'm sorry, but this is going to be a long, weird day."

"Awesome!" shouted my parents, then sipped their tea, eyes locked on me.

"Well?" asked Mum after pausing for a millisecond.

"Well what?"

"Who did it?"

"How would I know?"

"I thought maybe you'd figured it out," she said, deflated.

"You daft woman. It doesn't work like that. Max has to do his thing first."

"Then I'm putting my shoes back on. I don't want the nice police officers thinking I'm a hippy."

"The last thing the cops are going to think is a woman in a polka dot dress and red hair is a hippy. Especially…" Dad trailed off, clearly having realised whatever he was about to say was not too smart.

"Especially what?" she asked, stepping to him and fixing her stern frown on him.

Dad squirmed, then brightened and said,

"Especially because you're so pretty and so wonderful."

Mum melted into his arms and they sloshed tea as they kissed.

Turning away, I pulled out my phone, but was interrupted by a call from a woman approaching.

Anxious yipped, crawled out from under the VW, and tore across the field.

"Who's that?" asked Mum, full of suspicion.

"Joni Chin, one of the owners," I said.

"Jonichin?"

"No, Joni as in Joni Mitchell, and Chin as in the bit beneath your mouth."

Dad rubbed his chin and the lights went on. "Oh, that's Joni?"

"You didn't speak to her on the phone, I did," snapped Mum.

"So?"

"So, you don't know her. I never mentioned her name."

There was a confused silence for a moment, something I was used to with my folks, then Mum quickly slipped on her high heels because we had company, Dad smoothed down his T-shirt, ran strong hands through shiny hair, quickly used his steel comb he kept in his back pocket at all times, and they both stood to attention with their arms extended.

"Hi!" said Joni, warily looking from the two grinning statues to me.

"Hey, Joni. These two rather formal people are Jack and Jill, my parents."

"Jack and Jill? As in went up the hill?"

"Not following, love," said Dad happily.

"Me either," sang Mum, then flung herself at Joni and hugged her. Dad joined them, startling the poor campsite owner, causing Anxious to run around them, barking happily.

"Gosh, that was very... cuddly," said Joni once she was released.

"We're huggers," beamed Dad.

"We like to hug," agreed Mum.

"It's nice to meet you both. So, you got the caravan without any problems?" Joni glanced quickly at the monster, then caught my eye, trying to keep a straight face.

"Yes, and isn't it lovely?" asked my insane mother. "So bright and pink."

"It is very pink, yes." How Joni didn't laugh I will never know. "My lad sorted you out okay? He's so busy at work, but he promised he'd have it ready."

"Yes, no problems," said Dad.

I stared at them, incredulous. "How can you say that? What's wrong with you both? Everything is not okay."

"A problem?" asked Joni, frowning, clearly not wanting her guests to have any issues so soon after arrival.

"Joni, there's no easy way to say this, but there's a corpse in the caravan. A man. He's been cooked. Stewed, most likely. Possibly steamed."

Joni could be seen as a rather fierce woman. She was approaching fifty, with a shock of dark curly hair, a deep tan, and wrinkles from squinting. Five six in flat sandals, she wore work jeans, a simple vest, and clearly did plenty of manual labour around the campsite. Even though she was very thin, a bird of a woman, her forearms were muscular and her grip was firm. When she smiled, her eyes lit up and she was undoubtedly pretty, but she wasn't one to beat about the bush and spoke her mind. Right now, she was frowning, and her colour was up.

"I don't take kindly to jokes in such poor taste, Max. I know we've become friendly these past few days, but I don't like being ridiculed."

"Joni, I wouldn't joke about something like that."

"Max is telling the truth," said Dad.

"But you just said everything was fine," said Joni. "I

don't understand."

"We meant with the way the caravan looked," said Mum. "And it is very clean. But there is a dead man inside. He's naked. You can see his todger."

"His todger?"

"Yes, all men have them," explained Mum. "Willys. You know, the thing they—"

"Mum, I'm sure she gets it," I interrupted. "Come and see, then I need to call the police."

Joni stuck her head inside, gasped, staggered out, then slumped into a chair under the sun shelter. Once she got her breath back, she asked, "Do you know who it is?"

"No. We thought maybe you would. Or maybe your son? I'm guessing the police will want to talk to him and everyone else. Has anything like this ever happened before?"

"Of course not! Who would do such a thing? How could they? Why is he there? And why is there a tea towel over his head?"

"That's what my Max is going to find out," said Mum, tapping at her phone then thrusting it in Joni's face. "He's a real detective. Look, they wrote about him on the internet. He's got a wiki thingy."

"Do I?" I asked, intrigued despite the seriousness of the situation.

"I wrote it," said Dad proudly. "To keep track of your solved cases. That's five already and this will make six."

"You really solved those murders?" asked Joni, reading whatever Mum was showing her with interest.

"I did. Nothing like this, but I've realised it's my destiny. My vanlife is tied up with quite a few mysteries, and I've helped solve them."

"We helped too," piped up Mum.

"Then please help solve this terrible crime. We can't have people being murdered here. It'll give us a bad reputation. The Poach House lives by its reputation."

"Poach House?" I asked. "I thought the campsite was called The Poacher's Pitch?"

"Yes, but it's all part of the same business. The restaurant, pub, and our home is called The Poach House. That's the official name of the site."

"Bit of a coincidence," noted Dad. "If the guy in there has been poached."

"I hadn't thought about it until now," I admitted. "Sorry, I've been to so many campsites that I forget the names, and haven't been to the restaurant yet."

"Max likes to do his own cooking in his cast-iron pot," explained Mum.

"Yes, he told me. But you must come and try our food. My husband is a fine cook and as I said, this is our reputation on the line. What a disaster! And that poor man. Max, please help figure this out. We must call the police. But what will people think?"

"There's no avoiding it," I said.

"Then I'll phone them. Best I do it. I'm so sorry about this." Joni wandered off as she made the call, then returned and explained that the police said they were on their way.

"Better get the kettle on then," said Mum, humming as she banged about in my kitchen, destroying the order I'd worked so hard to maintain. She was many things, but neat was not one of them.

Chapter 3

By the time the police arrived, it was close to lunchtime. This was good for Joni as it meant the site was half empty now, with guests off exploring or hunting for somewhere to eat, but bad for us as we were hungry. It would have to wait a while.

As police cars, unmarked vehicles, ambulances, and a team of various experts descended, we remained under the sun shelter and watched the whole thing unfold. We were spoken to briefly to explain events, then ignored while the scene was photographed and a forensics team began their work.

And then we were told we had to leave. We were too close, the area needed to be kept secure, and they needed the space, but mostly I was convinced it was because Mum kept asking what they were doing, offering cups of tea, and generally getting in their way.

Joni appeared and suggested we go and have a bite to eat in the restaurant or the bar, the meal on her after the upset.

My folks jumped at the chance of a freebie, although I was less keen. Nevertheless, without even having given a proper statement yet, we joined Joni on the short walk across the campsite, through the gate, down the gravel car park and to the long, squat cottage that was both a home, pub, and restaurant. From the rear it wasn't too impressive, but from the roadside it was about as quaint a pub as you'd ever seen. Whitewashed stone, thatched roof, tiny windows, with bright displays in hanging baskets.

"Do you own the pub and campsite?" asked Dad.

"Yes. My husband took over many years ago. I actually used to work here when I was young, and that's how we met. He helped out in the restaurant then gradually became more involved, and we've both worked here ever since. His dad passed when he was young, so when his mother died he inherited and we took over and opened up the campsite. We both prefer running the camping side of things, but we can never keep a chef for long so now he's the cook. It's not ideal, but everyone has to make a living."

"You hear that, Max?" asked Mum. "Another chef."

"I haven't met him yet," I said.

"Bet he's not as good as our Max," said Dad.

"You can't say that!" I warned.

"Why not?" Dad pulled Joni to a stop and explained, "Max used to be at the top of his game. Michelin 3-star restaurants where they charged you an arm and a leg for a tiny serving of food on a slate or a board. Tasty, but you had to get fish and chips after to fill you up."

"We're not up to those standards," laughed Joni. "It's strictly pub grub, but it's homemade and the best in the area. Max told me about being a chef. We've had a few chats about things, but if you were so good, why leave?" she asked.

"It's complicated."

"He's obsessive. Once he gets into something, he won't let go. Always been the same," said Dad, happy to talk about me like I wasn't there. "Too focused. Single-minded."

"Yes, thanks for that," I said with a warning look he either ignored or didn't understand. I was never sure with him and Mum.

"Let's get you all inside and you can have something to eat and drink and hopefully they can sort out the mess at the caravan. I still can't believe this is happening. I hope they clear off before everyone returns later. It doesn't look very inviting as somewhere to stay."

"I'm guessing they'll be a few hours at least," I said.

"As long as they're gone by teatime." Joni strode off ahead, clearly stressed by the whole ordeal.

The pub interior was one of those gloomy small rooms that take you aback when you first enter. Cramped, with mismatched chairs, a low ceiling, a mix of original and print artwork covering every inch of wall, it clearly had a lot of history.

A few locals turned to stare, but most of the clientele were couples or families I spied through the doorway into a large dining room.

"Follow me," said Joni as she crooked a finger then marched off.

Anxious raced ahead, the smell of sausages strong in the air, so with a shrug to each other, we followed.

"Nice place," said Dad as he blocked the way and checked out the interior.

"Very cosy," agreed Mum, rubbing her hands together.

"Here we go," said Joni as she indicated a table. "Make yourselves comfortable and I'll be back in a few minutes. I need to check on my Dan. He's livid about this, but is so busy." Joni vanished into another small room which I assumed led to the kitchen.

"We should pay," I said as we took our seats.

"Why?" asked Dad. "She offered. It's rude to say no."

"Not this again." Mum shook her head, then picked up a menu and ignored us.

"You know I prefer to pay my own way and not be in anyone's debt. And if you don't foot the bill, you can't comment on the food. It's best to be in control."

"Son, it's a sandwich or some such, not a loan. Chill out."

Both studied the menu while I took a moment to familiarise myself with things. First was the smell. It wasn't wrong, but it wasn't great. I knew re-heated food when I smelled it. I detected less than perfectly fresh produce, overcooked veg, and burned meat. It was hard not to judge, and I was well aware that sometimes accidents happened in the kitchen, but it didn't smell quite right to my sensitive nose.

The handful of people eating didn't seem to have any issues tucking into baguettes or sausages in buns, even burgers or main meals, so maybe it was just me.

We decided to have the local sausages served in a crusty roll with a homemade ketchup and a side of French fries, maybe an extra few sausages for Anxious who was already getting antsy and utterly unconcerned by the smells in a negative way.

Joni returned with a man I assumed was Dan, her husband. An inch taller than me, he was very thin like his wife, with dark hair plastered to his pale skull, sunken eyes, and mean, downturned lips. Whereas Joni was mostly serious but smiled, too, Dan looked like he wouldn't even know how to turn his lips up instead of down. He was also wearing a dirty apron, which I disliked immensely. Knowing I was letting my old, obsessive ways about how things should be handled in commercial kitchens interfere with my judgement, I waited to see what was said and if I would re-consider my first impressions.

"You the bloke who keeps getting embroiled in murders, are you?"

"I guess," I said, smiling.

"Then don't go interfering with the coppers. I don't want no trouble. Leave them to their business and hopefully they'll sort this mess out before we go bust and are living on the roadside."

"Dan, be nice," soothed Joni, glancing at us and

smiling an apology.

"I'm just saying. We work hard and don't want any trouble."

"We didn't bring the trouble. It found us."

"You brought a cooked corpse onto our campsite."

"Maybe, or someone put it there after we arrived," I said, struggling to keep my cool.

"Yeah, well, it ain't right. I'll send the girl over for your order. Joni tells me it's on the house, so no main meal and no booze." Dan stomped his way back to the kitchen, the smell of burned meat trailing in his sour wake.

"Sorry about him," sighed Joni. "Dan's a sourpuss at times. He works very long hours in the kitchen when he'd prefer to be outside. He adores being a chef, but hates the lack of sunshine. He's a real outdoors person and sometimes he gets grumpy if he's been cooped up too long."

"Don't we all?" said Mum, surprising me by not saying anything mean about his attitude.

"Ignore what he said. You order whatever you want. It's on me for taking this upset so well."

"We'll all have the sausages, and can we have a few extra for Anxious? We'll sort out drinks in a moment," I said.

"Sure. I'll tell the waitress." Joni left with a weak smile, clearly pre-occupied.

"He's a bit of a grumpy bas—"

"Not too friendly." Mum interrupted Dad before he used bad language, something he rarely, if ever, did.

"I was going to say baster. Because he had one of those baster things in his hand," grumbled Dad.

"Why did he have that?" asked Mum.

"Maybe he's cooking more bodies and has one on the go?" chuckled Dad until he was silenced with a frown. "What? I was just trying to lighten the mood."

Our food arrived several minutes later, much to my parent's delight and my surprise. It looked and smelled fine, and tasted okay, but I knew kitchens and I knew the order was filled too quickly for any of it to have been cooked fresh and prepared with anything like any care or attention. I was also dubious about these being pork sausages. It tasted too gamey, although that might have been the seasoning.

The fries were lukewarm at best so I left mine, but Dad made short work of both portions, and Anxious had zero qualms about his sausages, so I said nothing and left everyone to enjoy their meal.

Joni arrived to clean away the plates, even though there was a waitress, but I think she was trying to stay busy until she heard from the police. When she returned from the kitchen an officer arrived, had a word, then left.

"He wants us to go and give proper statements. Apparently, they've finished with their initial investigation."

"Did they take the caravan away?" asked Dad, rubbing his hands together and grinning.

"I have no idea? Why?"

"Just asking," he said hurriedly as he ducked Mum's glare.

The campsite was busy with vehicles leaving, kicking up dust in the car park, the weather still as blistering as it had been all summer. I never thought I'd long for cool temperatures and rain, but Brits aren't used to such temperatures and it was playing havoc with everyone's conversation.

Normally focused on the cloud quality, the ferocity of the rain—focus on the fine drizzle that got you the wettest—and comparing it on a daily if not hourly basis, everyone had been stumped for months as all anyone could say was, "It's hot, isn't it?" and leave it at that. It just wasn't right.

People had returned after lunch and were being questioned at the campsite. I spied Mickey and Sue, the couple I'd met at the beginning of my campervan journey, but they were deep in conversation with an officer, so I'd catch up with them again later. We'd already spent a nice evening together, and had caught up on the gossip, but nothing quite like this. They'd been around earlier, but had kept their distance, and I hadn't told them what happened as things had moved too quickly.

Most vehicles had left the scene, leaving a pair of detectives who we'd yet to speak to, several officers, and a crime scene investigator packing up a considerable amount of equipment.

The officer led the way over to the pink abomination; he shielded his eyes, but kept looking back at us and shaking his head.

"He thinks I chose it," complained Dad.

"So? It's lovely. Apart from the corpse," said Mum.

The officer took Joni to one side and took her official statement while we approached a smiling pair of detectives sitting at the picnic bench sipping on drinks from shaker bottles. I was so taken aback by their friendly demeanour that I had to look behind me in case there was someone they knew there.

"Come and take a seat," said a squat, very trim woman with the widest smile I had ever seen. Her green eyes danced with mirth as she patted the bench.

"Don't be shy," laughed the man as he shook his drink, the metal mixer inside rattling. He looked like a bodybuilder rather than a detective, and I wondered if I'd been mistaken about who they were.

Apprehensive, we approached, and the woman patted the seat again. Up close, I noted that she, too, wasn't so much big as pure muscle. Both wore joggers with trainers, and sports T-shirts designed to allow the body to breathe. Hers was pink, his was a muted grey with black accents. Whereas she was pale and green-eyed, he was dark-skinned, most likely of Asian descent, with a trimmed moustache which, amazingly, suited him.

"Now, before we start, let me make the introductions," said the man, smiling at us then his partner. "We're both DSs. That means detective sergeants. Not the top brass, just workaday detectives, but we're the ones sent to check this out and will be running things unless it goes horribly wrong. That okay so far, folks?" His manner was bright, open, and unnervingly friendly. I liked him instantly.

"That sounds good to us," I agreed. "You aren't going to warn me to stay away from this and not get involved? Usually, I get told not to interfere, then sometimes the detectives start to trust me and don't mind me looking into things."

"Max, relax. We know all about you. We wouldn't be very thorough detectives otherwise," said the woman. "We checked you out, made a few calls, and yes, you have riled some of our fellow detectives. But they all admit you're smart. In fact, several said you were downright brilliant." She winked, then shook her drink and sipped it.

"Wow, okay. That's... good?"

"Yes, it is." She wiped the foam from her lips, the smell of chocolate protein powder strong. "I'm DS Sherry Hay, and this big lump of Indian muscle is Liam Ram. And before you ask, no, we are not a couple. We investigate hard, play hard, and work out hard together, but that's as far as it goes."

For some reason, they both found this hilarious and burst out laughing. I exchanged a confused shake of the head with my folks, although I had to hand it to Sherry, she had managed to keep them quiet for longer than anyone else I had ever known.

"Nice to meet you both," I said. "As you seem to already know, I'm Max, and this is Jack and Jill. The little guy keening for a fuss is Anxious."

"Aw, is he? What's the matter, buddy?" asked Liam, patting his lap.

As Anxious jumped up, tail wagging, and got a fuss from them both, I explained, "It's his name, not his state of mind."

"Right, of course," said Sherry happily, ignoring us

and teasing Anxious' ears in the way he loved. I knew that; how did she?

"So, here's what's going to happen," said Liam. "We'll ask you a lot of questions, you'll answer, then we'll most likely go over the entire thing again and again until you hate us, but then it's done and we'll be about our business. Shouldn't take too long, as from what I hear you just picked up the caravan, drove here, went for a walk, then discovered the corpse. Am I making sense so far?"

"Yes, absolutely." I checked on my parents as they still hadn't spoken, so I worried for their well-being. "You two okay?"

"Oh, phew! I thought we weren't allowed to speak," gushed Dad.

"Me too," said Mum, relief washing over her.

"Why?" I asked.

"I thought you weren't allowed to when the detectives were explaining," admitted Dad.

"That's what I thought!"

"So, you two work out, eh? Not bad, but look at these guns. Impressive, eh?" And just like that my crazy parents were back on form. Dad showing off his biceps, Mum quizzing Sherry about her workout routine, hardly letting the detectives get a word in edgeways.

Once they'd got it out of their system, we explained everything that had happened, and who we'd spoken to, if anyone. Mum and Dad promised they hadn't stopped on the way here after picking up the caravan, so either the body was already there or had been put inside here.

"Okay, so that all sounds reasonable. Now, let me explain where we're at," said Sherry.

"Really?" I asked, surprised.

"Sure. We'll keep you in the loop and expect the same in return. We know you're going to get in our way and visit people we want to question, so let's get real here. All we want is to solve this terrible crime, and that's what you want, right?"

"My Max is brilliant at solving murders," declared Mum. "And we helped with the first one."

"I did," said Dad. "I came up with the first clue."

"Then that's excellent." Sherry had the patience of a saint, and I couldn't believe how helpful they were both being. "Now, as to the body. There's no way of knowing who he is yet, but we're checking. More will be done now he's been taken by the medical examiner's team. Dental, fingerprints, maybe DNA. All that boring stuff. He's been dead a while, but no longer than a day, so that's good to know, right?"

We agreed it was, so I asked, "And he was stewed?"

"Stewed to the bone," said Liam, shaking his drink then finishing it off with a happy gasp. "Undercooked if anything, but yes, cooked. Most likely boiled or steamed. It's a head-scratcher, but we're good at our job and will begin our investigation now. The bods who know about these things reckon he was dead before he was cooked, but nevertheless, it's a peculiar thing to do. We'll have more soon and will let you know."

"Thank you for telling us. What could the motive be? I don't just mean the murder. I mean the stewing part?"

"Max," said Sherry, leaning forward and smiling, her green eyes flashing, "that's what we're hoping you can help us discover. You know cooking, so are one step ahead of us in that department. The only reason we can think of is some kind of industrial accident and someone tried to cover it up. But if that was the case, why dump the guy in a bright pink rental caravan? We still have people to interview and much to think about, but those are our initial thoughts."

"I had the same idea," I admitted.

"So did I," crowed Dad, puffing out his chest.

"No, you didn't," said Mum, slapping his wrist.

"I might have."

"I'm guessing an accident at a factory," I continued,

"but you're right, why put him in the caravan? The other option is they wanted him to be found. But again, why? The other theory is he wasn't dead when he went inside and was escaping someone, but he was too cooked for that."

"Or," said Mum, "someone planned on taking the caravan and disposing of him, but we got there and took it. We need to speak to the people at Sunny Parks."

"Good idea," I said, letting her think she was the first to come up with it. I winked at the detectives, who smiled, and after exchanging details, they packed up and were about to leave.

"Um, what about the caravan?" asked Dad with hope in his eyes. "Don't you need to take it away for forensics and as evidence and stuff?"

"Nope, all done. It's been gone over, photographed, and now it's yours again," said Sherry.

"Great. Just great," sighed Dad.

With that, we found ourselves alone, staring at the pink beast.

"How lucky are we?" crowed Mum, then skipped off happily over to the caravan and stood admiring it.

"I'm going on a cruise next time I want a break," sighed Dad.

"I might join you."

"No chance. If you do that, we'll be up to our necks in corpses before we even set sail."

I didn't argue; he was probably right.

Chapter 4

"That was weird," noted Dad.

"No, it wasn't," countered Mum.

"It was." I watched the detectives leave, then turned to my parents. "I've never met anyone like them before. Some of the police have been friendly, but they always warn me off. But they actually want us to help. They were so nice. And they aren't even new to the job. They seem to know what they're doing, are starting to follow up on leads right away, and yet they were fine with us poking our noses in."

"Max, not everyone is a grumpy old detective, sour and jaded by the job, or has something to prove. They were nice people," said Dad.

"Everyone ready?" Mum brandished a brand new pair of red and white Converse with fat laces she'd clearly taken the time to purchase so they matched her outfit.

"What are you talking about?" asked Dad.

"You heard the detectives. We can talk to anyone we like. You do both know who that is, don't you?" Mum grinned, a haughty, smug look as she thought she was one step ahead.

Being kind, I asked, "Who's that?"

"That boy at the rental place. Joni and Dan's lad. He rented us the caravan. He was in a rush, seemed pre-occupied, and Jack, did you notice how sweaty he was?"

"He was very sweaty, but it was very hot. Even hotter now. I'm burning up."

"That's a great idea, Mum. Well done!"

"Thanks." She beamed with pride, then tied her laces. When she stood and tested out her new footwear, she stared at my Crocs and ordered, "Put something less embarrassing on. I will not be seen out with my own flesh and blood in those monstrosities."

"They're practical for camping, and comfortable," I protested, knowing I was fighting a battle I could never win. "But for you, I'll change." I kissed the top of her head then sorted out a few things before turning to find them both about to enter the pink eyesore.

"You're going inside? Aren't you going to return it? I can't believe the police didn't impound it or something."

"Why would we take it back? It's still lovely. There's loads of room in there, and don't forget the pink kettle. I wonder if they left the tea towel?"

"How could we?" Dad shuddered, casting a worried glance through the open door. "I told your mother it's a freak mobile, but she insists we're keeping it."

"We paid, so we're using it!" Mum stamped her foot. There would be no more discussion.

"Why didn't they take it away?" I wondered. "Surely vehicles get impounded when they're part of a crime like this? It doesn't seem right."

"Maybe the detectives know something we don't," said Dad. "Maybe it's part of their plan to get the killer to reveal themselves. Might be a cunning ploy."

"Or maybe they checked it over, found nothing, just like the detectives said, so don't need it for anything," suggested Mum.

"Shall we take Vee? There's more room, as your car is still full of your stuff. Brought enough for the year, I see," I teased, noting the back seat piled to the roof with suitcases, boxes, and clothes in plastic.

"Just the essentials," bristled Mum.

"For about fifty normal people," grumbled Dad, winking at me.

"Are you saying I'm not normal?" She stepped to Dad and peered up while he found everything but her suddenly interesting.

"Course you are," I soothed, stifling a laugh. "But you're seriously going into the pink beast?"

"Don't you dare call it that! It's fine. I'm not scared." Mum grabbed Dad, shoved him through the doorway, jumped back, and waited.

When there were no screams, we both cautiously poked our heads inside. It smelled strange, of too many people, sweat, chemicals the teams had used, and the unmistakable tang of death.

"Better open up some windows, I think," said Mum brightly, then clattered around flinging open the small ventilation slits and running her hands over every available surface and item. We stayed by the door while she checked out the bedroom, calling out how cosy it was and that it would be lovely to have a cup of tea inside later.

Once she was done, we beat a hasty retreat, breathing deeply of the fresh air tinged with sweet aromas of freshly mowed grass.

"She's off her bleedin' rocker, that woman."

"At least she isn't freaked out."

"No, but I wish she was. I can't stay in that thing. Can I sleep in with you?"

"You're more than welcome, but we both know that isn't going to happen."

"No, she'll tan my hide if I leave her alone in there. But I won't sleep a wink."

I nodded, but knew that once his head hit the pink pillow he'd be out like a light. He could sleep on a bed of rocks and still wake up refreshed.

Anxious knew that mystery was afoot, so was keening to get on with things. Already settled on the bench seat in the back, he yipped for us to get a move on. Mum reluctantly left her garish nightmare on wheels and Dad locked up. Taking no chances in case he accidentally lost the keys, she stuffed them in her bag and we were good to go.

"Let's put some sounds on," called Dad from the backseat with a wicked grin once we'd pulled out of the campsite.

"Ooh, great idea. I brought a tape, as I know you're backwards with the technology in here." Mum fished about in her bag and pulled out what I knew would be a fifties mixtape.

"You guys want to listen to rock and roll while we're off to discover who stewed a stranger in your pink caravan?"

"Yes please!" they shouted.

Mum sorted out the music on the ancient cassette player in my van built only a few years before they were born, and we trundled through the lanes on a beautiful summer's day listening to a medley of fifties classics while my utterly content parents sang along to Elvis and other acts. Growing up, I learned all the famous names from a bygone era they were utterly obsessed with. If they weren't playing music, they were singing. If they weren't singing, they were dancing. Often, they did all three simultaneously.

Always with a smile, always with a kiss and a cuddle for each other, and always with their attention focused on our family. Being a teenager was not without its trials and tribulations. It took me a few years to get over the embarrassment of their style, and I hated to be seen in public with them because they were so different from other parents. Especially Mum, who never even left their bedroom without doing her hair and make-up and putting on a nice dress. But I soon realised that they were nothing to be ashamed of.

They were different, did what they wanted, and

refused to feel bad about not conforming. It was one of the best life lessons they ever gave me, and one I wished I'd taken to heart at a younger age than I had.

Now here we were, in my home on wheels, their son having finally learned this valuable lesson and gone his own way, done his own thing, and stuck it to the man.

"What are you smiling about?"

"Just thinking how great you both are. You're the best."

"Aw, thanks, love." Mum patted my hand and smiled happily. "Did you hear that, Jack?" she shouted, although there was no need. "Max said we're the best."

"We are," he hollered. "And he's a good lad. Get that woman back!"

"Don't you worry. This time next year, Min and I will be together."

"You better be. We miss her. She's like the daughter we never had. Although," he mused, "that would be weird if you married your sister. Maybe a cousin or something?"

"Yes, whatever you say," I agreed, feeling happy and pleased I'd asked them to come and spend time with me and Anxious. "Although, you know about the other thing I need to do, right? I explained the reason why I picked this spot to get together?"

"Course you did," said Dad. "I bet it's some numpty making a poor joke, but leaving notes in campervans making you believe someone's been kidnapped isn't funny as far as I'm concerned."

"Or me," said Mum with a scowl, crossing her arms for good measure.

"But I need to follow up on it. I've pretty much torn Vee apart looking for other notes. I had all the panels off, checked everywhere, and there's nothing else. But the two messages I did find need to be investigated. The police went to the owner's house, but he died not long after I bought Vee from him. His wife told them they mostly went away together but sometimes he did short trips alone. That doesn't explain how someone wrote a note saying they'd been locked up in there for weeks. It's bugging me and I need to speak to the wife."

"We're here for you, Son," said Dad. "Whatever you need."

"I figured it might be best if Mum speaks to the widow. You said that was okay, didn't you?"

"Of course. We'll go after we've been to the caravan showroom. Did you call her?"

"Yes, first thing, to check our visit was still okay. She was a bit weird on the phone, but said we could go. But for now, let's focus on this more pressing murder mystery."

"I can't believe we get to be part of two mysteries!" boomed Dad, causing Anxious to bark.

"I bet we solve them both before dinner," squealed Mum. "Then Max can make us one of his special one-pot wonders."

"I have the perfect dish in mind for this evening," I said with a wink.

We chatted away until I pulled up at the entrance to Sunny Parks. A massive swathe of gravelled wasteland reclaimed by the company and now a white sea of campervans, motorhomes of all sizes, and absolutely thousands of caravans either for sale or being looked after until the owners wanted them.

I parked in the visitor car park and we got out and stretched our legs. Judging by the size of the reception, this was a big business with a lot of money at stake, and they'd spared no expense. Steel and glass shone under the afternoon sun, and motorhomes costing as much as houses were lined up invitingly to the side, in a massive outdoor showroom.

Almost immediately, we were swarmed by eager salesmen and women, but Dad batted them off, Mum shooed them away, and I told them we'd speak to them once we'd had a look around.

Once alone, I bent to Anxious and told him to have

a good sniff around. He wagged as he focused on my pocket.

"Yes, there's a biscuit in it for you," I laughed.

Now knowing it was worth his while, he trotted off, nose to the ground, more than willing to oblige.

My parents explained that when they'd arrived they went into reception and the assistant came to get them a moment later. He'd been harried, didn't take too much notice of them, led them to the caravan where Dad groaned and Mum was beside herself, and more or less thrust the paperwork at Mum then gave them the keys. It was over in minutes.

"What's the son called?" I asked.

"Pete, or Paul, or was it Simon? Possibly Dave?"

"It was Mike," tutted Mum, rolling her eyes. "His name's on the paperwork."

"Then let's go find Mike," I suggested.

Rather than ask for him, we decided to walk around and get a feel for things. A surprising number of people were inspecting motorhomes or caravans, with a constant stream of owners coming and going, towing caravans. It was prime season, so the site was busy with owners collecting their homes on wheels, ready to embark on a trip.

Staff were everywhere, helping to find parked caravans, or showing what was on offer, and the smell of cash was strong in the air. Some of the prices were astonishing, but there were also plenty of secondhand vehicles at more affordable prices, and the size of some made me jealous. But none had the timeless style of my 67 VW.

Tucked away to the side of the building, a collection of more diverse offerings were lined up. Caravans in various colours, none as gauche as the pink crime against travel, beat-up campers, or retro motorhomes that had seen better days, these were more budget-friendly or available for rent. Some were clearly for weekend revellers or for those wishing to take something more unusual to a festival, and it was much more my thing.

"There he is," whispered Mum, pointing to the open door of a purple caravan where the rear of a man was poking out.

"How can you tell?" asked Dad. "Have you been staring at other men's bums again?"

"I have not! It's the trousers. They're black."

"So are all the staff's," I said.

"But his are, er... different. Come on." Mum surged ahead, so we hurried after her then waited while a man backed out of the tired-looking caravan with a bag of rubbish.

"Hi!" hollered Mum, causing him to jump around, face red, looking almost guilty.

"Er, hi. What can I do for you?"

"It's us, from earlier," pouted mum, hating it when people didn't remember her.

"Yes, of course. I recognise you," said Mike, eyes shifting to the caravan interior, then back to us. "Problem?"

"Yes, there's a problem," snapped Dad. "You rented us a caravan with a cooked corpse inside."

"Oh, er, yeah. Sorry about that."

"Are you taking the proverbial?" growled Dad, fists bunching.

"What? No, sorry. Let's start again. I just finished speaking to the police, and now I'm behind with work. I have to get this ready for a customer whose arriving any moment, and my boss isn't too happy. Bodies in caravans are bad for business." Mike smiled weakly, the strain evident. Like his father, he was tall, but unlike him he was running to fat already, with pasty skin, a wobbly belly with a white shirt tucked into plain black trousers, and small hands I knew were sweaty and soft.

"How old are you, Mike? And by the way, I'm Max."

"Eh? Oh, hey." We shook. His hand was soft and uncomfortably damp. Some would say moist! But not me.

"I'm twenty-six, why?"

"Just wondered. You didn't want to follow after your folks and work in the business?"

"Wanted to make my own way," he mumbled, eyes downcast.

There was clearly more to the story, but now wasn't the time. "Mike, if you spoke to the police, you know it's likely the victim was put in the caravan here. What can you tell us about that? Any insights? Ideas how it got there?"

"I swear it wasn't me!" he spluttered. "Like I told those detectives, I'd cleaned it out the day before. Right mess it was after a load of women had a party in it for three days. It was gross. Anyway, it was good to go. Mum had called and said this lady, Jill, wanted it, so I cleaned it up and never opened it again."

"Who had access to the keys?"

"The keys? Anyone here," he shrugged. "Staff, reception, manager, boss, anyone. We keep everything in the office on hooks. There's like, literally thousands of them. Every key has a number, and every vehicle is parked in that specific numbered bay. Otherwise it would be chaos. And before you ask, as the cops did, no, nobody is off work, nobody's missing, nobody hasn't turned up to collect a vehicle, and nothing weird has been going on."

"They were thorough," said Mum.

"They were."

Anxious returned, following a scent, only stopping when he bumped into Mike's shin. He looked up, sniffed his leg, then barked before sitting and turning to me, eyes on my pocket.

"Good job." I handed over his reward which he took gently, before settling down between us to enjoy it.

"Looks like the dog's found the guilty party," said Mum with her best glare.

Mike wilted under the intensity, the damp patches under his arms growing while she continued to pummel him with Mum eyes. He wiped his face, his eyes widening, as he gasped, "It wasn't me! He can just smell me because I cleaned out the caravan. I'm not a killer, and I certainly wouldn't know how to boil a whole person."

"So they told you about that?" I asked, surprised, but unsure why.

"Yeah. Nasty, eh?" he grinned, then licked his lips nervously.

"What's so amusing, lad?" asked Dad.

"Nothing. But it's so boring around here and now we have a crazed murderer on the loose. My guess is it's from the factory. Look, they're always belching smoke or steam or something. I bet someone from over there did it. It's the ideal setup to get away with murder."

"What is that place?" I asked.

"Ah, wouldn't you like to know?" he asked slyly, smiling.

"Yes, that's why he asked," said Dad. "Are you alright, lad? A bit slow on the uptake, are you? That's alright, not everyone's smart."

"What? No, I was just teasing. And I am smart. I have this job, and I'm working my way up the ranks. Soon, I'll be selling motorhomes and raking in the cash. You just wait. I'm gonna be rich, and that'll show my parents."

"Okay, no need to get your knickers in a twist. You don't have to prove anything to us." Dad patted Mike on the shoulder, then removed his hand and stared at his palm.

"No, just to my parents. They said I would never handle it here. Wanted me to be a waiter or cut the grass or something. I've never been good with numbers, so they wouldn't let me work behind the bar, and I really wanted to be in the kitchen, but now I'm showing them."

"Sure you are," soothed Dad. "Now, what's the factory for?"

"Oh, didn't I say? It's the sausage factory. Mostly hotdogs, or Frankfurters, whatever you want to call them."

I groaned, but it was too late. Anxious, who had been utterly pre-occupied with his biscuit, sprang to attention, began barking manically as he ran around in circles, sniffing, searching, looking everywhere for the source of his favourite meaty treat.

"I think we better go pay them a visit," I sighed, knowing he'd never settle until this was done. Also doubting this was a coincidence. If they processed pork, and made hotdogs, then surely they had the means to stew a person?

Chapter 5

"Anxious, stop barking," warned Mum. "We're going to the sausage factory in a minute."

"Don't say it!" we shouted, but it was too late. At the words, he increased his speed, upped the decibels, and was soon close to hyperventilating.

"Oops!"

"Thanks for the heads-up, Mike," I said, then nodded and hurried off before Anxious collapsed.

Mum and Dad followed right on our heels, clearly not keen to remain in Mike's company any longer either.

"There's something off about that lad," whispered Dad, glancing back. "Now he's waving. What's that about?"

"He's a funny boy," agreed Mum. "He's trying to prove he can be independent, that's all. Nothing wrong with that." Dad and I both screeched to a halt and stared at her. "What?"

"You refused to let me leave home unless I promised to call every day, bring my dirty clothes for you to wash once a week, and swear on Dad's life that I would never meet a girl."

"Don't be silly. That was just me joking around." Mum fiddled with her bandanna, pulling it down almost over her thick lashes.

"Really? When I told you about Min, you said she better not take me away from you and that you would only meet her if I promised she was going to be my wife."

"That's different. I didn't want to meet one of your floozies."

"Since when did I have floozies? You know I was never like that."

"You could have been up to all sorts. Playing the pitch, up to no good."

"It's playing the field," corrected Dad.

"Is it?"

"Yes, but Max is a good boy. You got free of us in the end, though, didn't you?" He winked, knowing what Mum was like.

"Never," I laughed.

Anxious was scratching at the door to Vee—good job I wasn't too precious about the paintwork, but it still made me wince—so I hurried to open up then we piled in.

It wasn't difficult to find the sausage factory as the steam, at least I hoped it was, belching from the large metal stack made it impossible to miss. At least it was out of town, but I was sure the locals would have something to say about such an unsightly blot on the landscape. Although, sometimes such things were welcome, as at least factories brought jobs to the community.

When I entered the cramped car park, I was surprised to find how small the actual factory was. Rather than a sprawling behemoth of an industrial-sized operation, it was a rather squat, single-story, white metal-clad building with an array of solar panels on the roof. The edifice had a tired, past-its-best air about it, although it was clearly well-maintained.

Only a handful of vehicles were present, leading me to believe that much of what went on inside was automated. We took a moment to study the building, then walked around to the side where three loading bays were empty. The rear was nothing but a grassy area with seating for staff and a gazebo for when the weather was either inclement, or like today, too hot to stand out in the sun.

We hurried back to the entrance, thankful for the shade of the porch, then went inside. The door creaked horribly as it closed slowly behind us. Cheap carpet almost worn to the concrete floor gave the interior a dated, uncared for feel on first impression, but it was light, surprisingly airy, and smelled of lemon rather than raw meat.

A pretty receptionist with a shock of pink hair looked up from her monitor and smiled at us.

"Hi! How can I help you? Have you come for the tour?" she asked with rather too much enthusiasm.

"Ooh, a tour," gushed Mum, hurrying forward, always drawn to anyone with hair as adventurous as her own. "I've always wanted to go on a tour of a sausage factory."

"Since when?" I asked.

"You've never mentioned it in your life," said Dad, bustling past me and almost shoving Mum out of the way so he could thrust his hand out and greet the receptionist. "I'm Jack, this is Jill, and that's Max. We'd love to do the tour. What time does it start? Do we have to pay?"

"Actually," she confided, leaning forward, causing me to rush over and us to lean forward, "whenever you want. Nobody ever comes for the tour, so we'd love to have you. It's my first one, but don't tell anyone. And it's free! Good news, eh?"

"Mum's the word," said, er, Mum.

"The word for what?" asked the young girl, clearly many generations removed from the rest of us.

"It's a saying, love," said Dad. "It means your secret is safe with us."

"Oh, right!" she said brightly. "I'll just get my hair net. You all have to wear one, and I'm afraid no dogs are allowed. Health and safety and all that. Might contaminate the hotdogs. We do the best ones in the area. All the local shops stock them, and we make thousands a day. But gosh, listen to me giving away the fun facts. Let's save it for the tour, shall we?"

"Can't wait," said Mum, rubbing her hands together.

"No, it'll be thrilling," said Dad with a wink to me and a shake of his head directed at Mum.

"Awesome," said the now hopping receptionist as she tried to put blue elasticated bags over her trainers. "Help yourselves to nets and the footwear protection. We don't want anything to get into the hotdogs apart from prime British outdoor reared pork!"

"Sorry, love, we didn't catch your name," said Dad as he sat on the floor then pulled on the foot protection before scowling at Mum as he dragged the net over his perfectly quiffed hair.

"Gosh, how rude of me," she giggled. "I'm Tracy. No e."

"Tracy Noee?" asked Dad. "That's an unusual surname."

"I didn't tell you my surname. It's Smith. That's not odd."

"You said it was Noee!"

"Dad, she meant she spells Tracy without an e after the c."

"Then why didn't she say so?"

"She did, you big lump of denim-clad dippyness," scolded Mum with a wag of her finger.

"Yes, well, is everyone ready?" asked Tracy.

"Almost," I said, pulling on my own protective gear then turning to Anxious who was standing stock still, tail down, ears flat to his head, eyes like saucers as he stared at the magical doors to all his Christmases come at once.

"Are you sure he can't go in?" asked Dad. "Look how sad he is. He's only little. Maybe just for a minute?"

"No dogs allowed or I'd be out of a job."

I bent to the little guy and promised, "I'll bring you a lovely treat. A nice pack of sausages just for you. How does that sound?"

Anxious drooled, but whined, pawing at my knee, pleading to be let into paradise.

"I know it's tough, but it's character building." Turning, I asked Tracy, "Can he wait in reception?"

"Sure, as long as he doesn't make a mess."

"Great. Won't be long, buddy. Be good." After cuddling him, his warm body trembling, I reluctantly stood and followed the others through the double doors into a very clean, very quiet, very empty factory.

"There's no smell," noted Dad.

"Raw meat shouldn't smell," said Tracy. "It's a common misconception, but our meat is as fresh as possible and is processed quickly, so next to zero smell. If you would care to look up, you will notice the large extractors dotted around the factory. They ensure the environment remains pristine and free of any odours or contaminants. Even the smokers, which give the hotdogs that familiar taste, have built-in extractors so nothing else becomes tainted." Tracy was warming to her first ever tour, and had learned the spiel well.

We hung back for a moment and agreed not to ask about the stewed body and complete the tour first before bringing up the subject, so for the next half an hour we were told in excruciating detail about how each machine worked, the ingredients, although not the secret ones, and given a potted history of the company. There was also a lengthy interlude where Tracy rather forgot herself and started complaining about her mum and how she should be allowed to choose the channels on the TV at least sometimes now she was a grown-up and had a proper job.

Finally, the tour was complete, and we finished at the last machine, having only seen a handful of people the entire time. Two women kept an eye on the packing process, an elderly man ran the actual machine for making hotdogs, and a big, burly man seemed to do the rest, including handling the smoking. He loaded up the machines, but also unloaded the deliveries with a forklift truck, which is where we found ourselves now.

"And that concludes the tour!" sang Tracy, rather flushed and her voice rising in pitch. "How did I do?"

"Brilliant," said Mum, sounding like she actually meant it. To be fair she had done a fine job; it simply wasn't very interesting. Mum began to clap, so Dad and I joined in and Tracy was delighted.

"Gosh, thank you so much. I'll leave you in the capable hands of our most indispensable employee and all round great guy, Jason." Tracy turned to him where he'd been waiting impatiently, leaning on a stack of boxes, and said, "Over to you, Jason." Tracy smiled once more, waved vigorously, then scuttled back to reception, where Anxious would no doubt be pleased to have company for a few minutes.

"So, what do you want to know?" asked Jason, a swarthy guy with a bushy beard, a shaved head, and a body any bouncer would be proud of. If he wanted to act disinterested, he'd be up for an Oscar.

"You seem to do most of the work around here," I began, "so I'm assuming you know everyone and how everything works?"

"Sure," he shrugged, glancing at a pallet half loaded with boxes.

"We won't keep you long, and it's too cold in here anyway, but here's the thing. Do you have staff missing who should be in work?"

"Nope. Although the night staff aren't here, obviously. This is a twenty-four-hour operation. And weekends. Non-stop, it is."

"Oh. Have you heard about anyone disappearing?"

"Blimey, not this again? You're too late, mate. The cops beat you to it. They've already been and gone. You just missed them. Snooping, are you? You that bloke they warned me about?"

"I guess I am. But we aren't snooping. We're trying

to help. Anything you can tell us? A man was cooked, and you have the equipment to do that here, don't you?"

"Nothing like that, no."

"You do. We saw it," said Dad.

"It's possible," admitted Jason, "but you'd have a right job getting a body in and out. Especially without being seen. Not anyone who could do that. And then what? You drag the poor guy through the factory and out the loading bay? Not very likely, is it?"

"Not very," I admitted. "What did the police think? Did you show them the steamer?"

"Sure. And they said the same thing as me. That it's too high, too awkward, and this isn't where it happened. Look, are we done? I have a guy waiting to be loaded and it's just me."

"Yes, sorry to hold you up."

Shivering, we left him in the cool room and walked freely through the factory, heading to reception.

"Are we allowed to be here?" asked Mum, looking nervous.

"Course we are," said Dad, "or we wouldn't be here."

"That's not a reason," sniffed Mum. "We might get into trouble."

"Let's have another quick look at the steaming machine," I suggested.

We hurried over, having not had much chance to study it on the tour, but there wasn't that much to be seen. A large machine steamed the smoky sausages a little as they passed through a huge cylinder on its side, but there was no way to get a person in there that I could see, and with the various safety features it was a no-go.

"This is a dead end, I think," I admitted.

"Shame. It would have been nice to solve it before dinner," sighed Mum.

"Never mind, love. It just means we get to carry on later and tomorrow."

"True."

I took in the rest of the factory, wondering if any of the other processing machines would work, but only the steamer made sense. Eventually, I had to admit that none of it seemed very likely, as the factory was set up for processing links of smoked Frankfurter type sausages, not huge man-sized amounts of meat.

Back out in reception it was eerily quiet. No Tracy, and no Anxious.

"Where is he?" I whispered.

"Maybe Tracy took him for a walk," said Dad, shrugging.

"Why would she do that? She should be working," said Mum.

"I don't know," admitted Dad.

"We better check back inside," I said, getting a sinking feeling.

I hurriedly opened the door and a blur of white and brown sped past, too fast for me to recognise Anxious, but it was either him or a very large rat.

"Anxious!" I hissed. "Come here."

He was nowhere to be seen, so I ran after him but when I got past a machine he'd vanished. Thinking it through logically, meaning, thinking with my belly, I made a beeline for the production line where the racks of hotdogs were snipped into singles on the rolling conveyor belt. If I were a desperately starving dog, that's where I'd be headed.

Racing over, smiling at the shocked workers, I spied my greedy pooch as he was readying to launch onto the machine and fill his boots. If he did that, the entire batch would be ruined, the machines would have to be shut down, and everything thoroughly cleaned.

I ducked low, and ran for it, sweeping past him as he sprang, tongue already out, ears flapping, and scooped him up into my arms before he touched anything.

Landing with my arms outstretched, flat on my

stomach, I was defenceless against the excited licking that ensued until I managed to clamber to my feet with him held firmly in my grasp.

"You could contaminate the hotdogs," I warned. "And you shouldn't eat these ones as they have quite a lot of salt. We'll get some of the raw sausages they also make and cook them at home this evening. You were very naughty."

For a millisecond, Anxious was sad, then he resumed his licking, drooling as he thought about the feast to come. Concealing him as best I could, I skirted around the edge of the factory floor away from anyone and stepped through into reception just as Tracy appeared from a side door.

"Oh, hi! Just nipped to the loo. Everything okay? I thought you'd left."

"We were just about to. Thanks again for the tour," I said, ushering my parents out before they gave the game away, which was pretty much guaranteed.

After handing Anxious over, I popped back inside and bought a few packs of sausages and a jar of the Frankfurters, then left Tracy to her work.

With Anxious safely stowed in the back, eyes locked on the fridge containing bliss in sausage form, we buckled up and returned to the campsite to the sound of my parents belting out several upbeat rock favourites and Anxious howling. Whether in protest or singing along, it was hard to discern the difference, but I knew which one I'd put my money on.

Entering the campsite felt like coming home, and I couldn't get out of the van fast enough. The others felt the same, and we sank into our chairs with a sigh. Anxious lay between them, always happy when they were around. Never quite understanding why his favourite people apart from me kept coming and going.

I often wondered if this life was right for him, but had realised that he adored it. He had his routines based around the campervan, our kitchen, and the day-to-day activities that were done regardless of where we were, but he revelled in the freedom like he'd never had before, and adored meeting new people.

I laughed when I realised I could have been describing my own feelings on the matter, causing my folks to stare at me quizzically.

"Sorry, I was just thinking about Anxious and if this is the best life for him. Then I had an epiphany. It's right for him, and me. We love it."

"You're a lucky man," said Dad, serious for once. "It's not for everyone, certainly not for us for more than a few days, but vanlife has a lot of positives. Being outside is where we're all meant to be, not stuck inside stupid little boxes. And yes, I know some people love that, but there's nothing like fresh air and seeing the country. You made the right choice, Max. Now, put the kettle on, let's have a brew, then we'll go and chat with the woman you arranged to meet."

Mum stirred, having dozed off, and asked, "What woman?"

"The wife of the man Max bought the campervan from. You're going to woo her with your feminine wiles and get her to tell us everything."

"Too right I am," said Mum. "I'll woo her until my wiles wither." She nodded, then closed her eyes.

Dad shook his head at me and smirked, pleased to have me around to share his utter bemusement at how she behaved sometimes, but I knew he wouldn't have it any other way. I wouldn't either.

Chapter 6

After a cup of tea, I prepped a few ingredients for the evening meal while the fifties nuts took Anxious for a nice walk. The silence was divine.

I'm sure all children, be they sixteen or sixty, feel the same about their parents. They love them, would do anything for them, but after intense time together it's always nice to have a moment to gather your thoughts.

There was certainly plenty to mull over.

Mike, the son of the owners here, clearly had something to prove to them. From what I could surmise, he wasn't cut out for life here, but was struggling to make a go of it at Sunny Parks. After working there for some time, he was yet to move up to a more lucrative sales position. That obviously rankled. Did that make him a murderer? Of course not. But it certainly made him a suspect, albeit a foolish one for putting himself directly in the line of fire.

I knew better than to rule anyone out, though, as people never ceased to amaze me with their sense of infallibility or downright dumb behaviour. The hotdog factory niggled at me, mostly because of the industrial-sized steamers and ovens, but how on earth could someone have got a body in and out? And if no workers were missing, who was the unfortunate victim? I'd have to check again tomorrow to see if everyone had turned up, but even if they had that still might mean one of them had done the deed and we were yet to uncover who was killed.

Chopping vegetables allowed me to find a quiet, still place inside, and examine what my instincts were telling me. I was missing something here, but it was early days, and the truth was yet to present itself. The best approach was to use my attention to detail honed over years working in fine-dining restaurants where absolutely everything mattered, and to let what I experienced percolate in my subconscious until the truth finally clicked.

Checking my watch, I was pleased to note we still had a few hours before I needed to get dinner on as we wouldn't eat until seven or later tonight. The warm, light evenings meant that anything too early left you in a pool of sweat, wondering why you didn't just have a cold salad, and that was no way to live! Salads were all well and good, but the star of the show? Never!

Old habits died hard, so I wiped down the counter, put the raw ingredients into Tupperware and stowed it in my fridge. It was the one thing I disliked about my campervan, as a man obsessed with food and always trying to pick up the best local ingredients needed a full-sized one, preferably with a separate freezer, but I knew the challenge had been good for me. I was much more mindful of my choices, and certainly cut out most processed food or anything I didn't absolutely need.

With tea towels folded, the damp ones and the cloths wrung out then pegged onto the small line I always put up so things could dry out and not make the van smell funky, I stepped back, grunted my satisfaction at the order I had created, if only until Mum began rooting around for something, then turned and stared at the pink behemoth. Reluctantly, I actually took the time to study it properly rather than avert my gaze for fear of a life-sized plastic Barbie doll staggering out with an axe raised.

"It really is very pink," I chuckled, shaking my head at Mum's choice of accommodation.

Besides the startling colour, it was the shape that

was truly bizarre. Chrome bumpers and trim seemed to have been added almost randomly, providing neither protection from collision—it was being towed, after all—or anything redeeming in terms of design.

With oversized brake lights and indicators, it was more akin to a rotund, otherworldly alien blob than anything else. It was too wide, too tall, too everything. Even that wasn't what made it plain wrong. Something was almost screaming at me, but I couldn't explain it. Was it bigger on the outside than the inside? Or the other way around?

Scratching my head, I reluctantly opened the door and stepped inside. A tentative sniff revealed the funky smells had gone thanks to the open windows, so I secured the door on the latch to keep it open, having palpitations for a moment imagining getting stuck inside if the door banged shut and my folks decided to go on an extra long walk, leaving me entombed in pink hell, then took in the room.

All was as it had been. Mum and Dad hadn't even unpacked yet, and although the place had been disrupted by the police and associated teams, there wasn't that much they could do to mess things up. Moving back to the door, I bent, then stretched out my arms as though dragging a heavy object inside. How would the killer have done it?

The victim was average size, although a little overweight, so he would certainly have been difficult to move. Trying to drag a corpse up the two metal steps would be awkward, and then he would have been pulled across the floor and dumped.

The other option was that he was carried. Such a weight would be a struggle, but not impossible to manage. I could certainly give a grown man a fireman's carry. Have the body over my shoulder, duck awkwardly to get through the door, then drop him? Was that what happened?

A few things began to make sense. Plenty didn't. Fingerprints were nigh on impossible to trace according to the detectives, as although Mike had done a thorough job of cleaning the caravan there were literally scores of them.

Most were partials, some complete, but with hen parties, and various groups having used the caravan it was a mammoth job trying to trace them all and the police had dismissed it as unlikely to lead to the killer. Whoever had done this would have worn gloves unless they were so tied to the caravan, like Mike or his co-workers, that it would have been more strange if their fingerprints weren't present.

With a final glance at the interior, I spied a strange scuff on the ceiling. Moving in for a closer look, I noted that the material lining the ceiling had been torn then repaired, most likely just glued back into place. Hardly having to rise on tip-toe, I sniffed the almost imperceptible tear line, and got the unmistakable whiff of glue.

Rowdy groups of women out for a wild few days to celebrate a forthcoming wedding might have easily caused a little damage, but Mike hadn't mentioned the repair. Then again, why would he? Stowing it away as a possible clue, I retreated to the free world, flashes of pink strobing across my vision as I closed the door.

"Hello, love," said Mum with a confused smile as I turned.

"Hey. Good walk?"

"Great," said Dad. "There are some nice views from up the hill, and it isn't too steep. Anxious had a great time chasing after rabbits."

"You shouldn't encourage him," tutted Mum. "Those poor things might get eaten."

"He never tries to hurt them. It's a game for him. I don't encourage it, but Anxious has been chasing rabbits since a puppy. It's part of the Terrier nature."

"Max, that's no excuse. What if he caught one?"

"He never has yet. And the one time he came up against a rabbit that didn't run he put his tail between his legs and scarpered back to me."

"See. I told you it was fine." Dad wagged a finger. "Now, are we going straight off?"

"We haven't unpacked, and I haven't done my hair

or changed my dress or even looked in a mirror!"

"Mum, you look lovely," I said. "How about we go talk to this lady, then when we return you can sort your things out and I can make dinner?"

"You've got a deal," said Dad hastily.

"Yes, I suppose that'll be fine," huffed Mum, glancing with longing at her clothes in the car.

After Anxious had a drink and we took a few minutes to ready ourselves, we set off for the second time. It was turning into a very busy day, not what we'd expected at all, and yet we had plenty of the afternoon left. I still found it hard to reconcile the severity of the crime with the speed the scene was investigated then released, but had to remind myself that other similar crimes had been gone over rather rapidly too. With so much based around video recordings and photographs now, I supposed it was the way these things worked, but it never had seemed quite right to me.

"Are we there yet?" boomed Mum from the back, having decided she wanted to cuddle up with Anxious rather than be asked about directions.

"Yes, Mum, we're there."

"Are you being sarcastic?"

"No. Are you?"

"I don't think so."

"Good." I winked at Dad and we enjoyed the silence for a while as I followed the directions I'd put into my phone.

After only fifteen minutes we were almost there. I tried not to think about what I was going to ask, as I wanted this to be a casual conversation, not an interrogation, and as we'd arranged, Mum would take the lead, putting the woman at ease and working her magic. She could chat to anyone, and got people to say things they would never dream of mentioning to anyone else. It was simply her way.

"Everyone ready?" I asked as I pulled up outside a

fifties semi-detached house on a quiet suburban street.

"Sure," said Dad. "I hope you get the answers you're looking for, but if the police have already spoken to this woman, do you think you'll get any information from her?"

"I hope so. I can't shake this off, you know? Those notes are worrying me, and I can't leave this alone until I'm satisfied this was just a very peculiar joke. I want Mum to find out what kind of man he was. Was he a practical joker, or a serious guy? Would he do something like this to wind me up? Or could he have genuinely kidnapped someone without his wife knowing about it?"

"Leave it to me," trilled Mum, banging about as she stood.

"I'm not so sure this is a smart idea," I sighed, starting to worry that Mum would insult this lady and it would go horribly wrong. She may have been able to talk the hind leg off a donkey, and got on with people, but if she took a dislike to someone she wasn't afraid to share that information with the focus of her scorn.

"Too late now," chuckled Dad as he slapped me on the back.

"Yeah, I guess so."

We went up the generous drive, noted the expensive and very large motorhome parked next to a red Mini Cooper, then I knocked.

A few seconds later, a woman in her sixties with a ready smile and a shock of spiky white hair answered the door.

"You must be the new owner of the camper," she said, keeping her smile in place but clearly confused by her visitors. My folks had that effect on most people, and for good reason.

"I am. Hi. We spoke on the phone and you said it was okay to bring my parents along. They're visiting with me and we thought it best if you speak to Mum. This friendly guy is called Anxious, but he can wait outside if it's a bother."

"Nonsense. You're a cute one, aren't you?" Olive's face lit up as she bent easily to Anxious and stroked him, while the little guy had a sniff of her leg, then ushered us inside.

We removed our shoes and lined them up on the mat beside the door, then followed Olive down a simple hallway with family pictures on the walls, a large gilt-framed mirror, and several ornaments on a console. The unmistakable smell of new carpet was strong, a peculiar chemical tang that took weeks to work its way out. The carpet was expensive, cream, and real wool as far as I could tell, and a joy to walk on.

The living room had the same carpet, and we were directed to a shabby brown sofa in the neat, very orderly room, where the main focus was clearly the large TV mounted on the wall, the flat screen gleaming after a thorough polish.

"It's old, but comfortable," said Olive as she indicated we take a seat. She perched on the armchair and leaned forward, eager for us to speak.

"Thanks for letting us talk to you," said Mum in her best posh voice. Something she always did when meeting people she wanted to impress. "I'm Jill, and that's Jack. You have a lovely home. I adore the carpet. Is it new? Axminster, isn't it?"

"Yes, thank you. Just laid last week. After my Noel passed, I'm afraid I went spend-crazy. We always poured our money into trips away, but now I'm home more I actually took proper notice of the house for the first time in years. It's rather dated, so I'm slowly updating things."

"Nothing wrong with some retail therapy," said Mum. "Was it sudden? Him passing, I mean. Not buying the carpet."

Olive laughed, Mum's ability to tone down her words working. "Yes, quite sudden. He was only sixty-four, and very fit. We were always hiking and cycling or away in the camper, and we figured we had decades together yet.

Then he got ill and died. Heart attack, but he recovered, then he seemed to be better and was taking it easy but had another one. He died right there." Olive pointed to a spot by an old-fashioned gas fire, the three bars clean but it clearly wasn't used as it was disconnected from the inlet valve.

"Hence the new carpet?" I asked.

"Yes. Exactly. Sorry, where are my manners? Shall I make tea, or would you prefer coffee? I can do soft drinks too. I always have loads in for the grandchildren."

We asked for tea, so Olive excused herself while we studied the room and waited. None of us spoke, not wanting to be overheard, so instead just watched Anxious as he kept returning time and time again to a ceramic ornament collection on the hearth, unable to work out if he should bark at miniature horses or lick them. In the end, he settled for a sniff and a lick, then curled up on the rug, groaned, and closed his eyes. He clearly didn't feel like anything was wrong here, but the smell of the carpet stopped him from investigating much.

Once we'd been given our tea, Mum broached the sensitive subject of the notes. "I'm sure the police told you about the messages my Max found in the campervan?"

"A terrible business. So horrid."

"But you didn't know anything about them until the police asked?"

"Of course not! I would never do such a terrible thing. And neither would my Noel."

"Can you think of anyone who might?" I asked. "Other friends or family? Any children that might have been playing in the van and thought it would be funny? Maybe pretend they were being kidnapped? Something simple like that?"

"There are grandchildren, of course, and nieces and nephews from both sides with their own children who have been in and out of the van over the years, but I can't imagine any of them hiding away messages like that. I've spoken to everyone in the family and nobody was anything but shocked."

"They would be, yes," soothed Mum. "Now for the most delicate question, and please understand we mean no offence. Could your Noel have kidnapped somebody?"

"Never!"

"He didn't go away alone in the campervan?"

"On occasion, but like I said to the police, never for longer than a weekend away. It was something we mostly did together, although not as much over the last few years. He was obsessed with VWs, and upgraded once he sold to Max, but a lot of time, effort, and money went into the van. He had it for a long time, and adored the old thing. When he got it, it needed considerable work, even though the previous owner had it from new. He'd spend every spare minute bringing it up to scratch. We both adored it. But as we got older, we wanted something with more space. And my poor Noel never got to use the new van much at all."

"Where is it?" I asked.

"I sold it. It brought back too many memories, so I bought something totally different. The modern motorhome doesn't have the same intimate feeling, and it isn't as pretty, but the room inside is very welcome. I've only had a few trips as I'm alone now and it isn't the same, but I'll take a long trip soon. I do love the vanlife."

"Me too," I agreed, smiling at Olive who was fidgeting with the edge of a cushion she'd placed in her lap.

"Where would he go if he travelled alone?" asked Dad. "Any favourite spot? And one more thing. Was there a time when the van wasn't here for a while? In for repairs somewhere maybe?"

"Why, yes, every year it would be in the garage for weeks at a time. The police never asked that, actually. Noel was fanatical about getting it serviced and everything checked over, so took it to a specialist. They were always slow, and I kept telling him to use someone else, but he was happy with the work, so I mostly kept out of it. It usually took him hours to drive to the silly place. He liked to take his time, and stop off for a bite to eat, so he'd stay over in a hotel then return the next day. Sometimes the day after. Then the same when he picked it up. It gave us a break from each other, and he worked so hard. Not that we had any marital issues, you understand?"

"Of course," I agreed. We looked at each other, but said nothing more.

"Who did the servicing?" I asked.

Olive stood and fished around in a drawer then pulled out an oily card and handed it to me. "You can take it. I won't use them. I don't want my van gone for weeks. The place around the corner does fine work and they said they can do motorhomes if anything goes wrong, so I'll use them."

"But Noel never did?"

"No, he liked to go with people who were as keen on VWs as us. But they were too slow. And as to where he went on trips without me, it was one of our favourite places. But sometimes we needed a day or two apart, or I just didn't fancy it, so he'd go alone. A nice spot in the middle of nowhere we discovered on a walking holiday, with a lovely village nearby. Kendal Wood, it's called. There's no campsite there, but it's easy to find if you follow the directions. About an hour from here. I can tell you how to get there."

"Thank you for telling us. If you show me on my phone, that would be perfect."

After I got all the details I needed, we exchanged pleasantries for a few more minutes, then thanked Olive for her time before leaving.

Back in the van, and with everyone settled, I asked, "Well?"

"He obviously had someone locked up when he was pretending the van was at the garage. Bit of an oversight by the police not asking if the van was gone for ages." Dad grinned, pleased with his detective work.

"They were focused on him being with the van,

rather than just the van. I think we need to check out this garage."

"Can't you call them?" asked Mum. "I'm getting tired and time's getting on. Or go tomorrow?"

"Sure, Mum. It has been a very long day. Maybe we should unwind and forget about this for a while? I'm sorry to drag you into another mystery, but this was why I came to the area, and if I don't do it now I never will."

"Son, that is so not true. One thing we all know is that once you get hold of something you never let go until you're satisfied."

"He's like a bulldog," agreed Mum. "Just a very handsome one."

"You do know that when your mum tells you how handsome you are it doesn't count, right? Sons know you're biased. If I had a massive boil on my nose, you'd say it was a lovely beauty mark."

"But you are handsome," protested Mum.

"Thanks. You did really well with Olive. But why the posh voice? I bet it was killing you to not speak normally and give her the third degree."

"It was draining."

"That's why you're so tired," said Dad. "It's not the murders and the mystery. It's having to sound posh for ten minutes and reign in your gabbing."

I drove home to jovial bickering and the raucous caterwauling of Chuck Berry.

Chapter 7

Anxious was famished, so I fed him a partial bowl of his dinner early then began cooking, my focus on the food. The portable stove had a new gas bottle so the pressure was different and I panicked something might burn, so kept a watchful eye on the pot for a few minutes once everything was simmering away nicely, then relaxed with my folks and had a glass of wine.

The air had cooled somewhat, and although still hotter than most daytime temperatures, it was pleasant, and soon our conversation died as we soaked up the unique atmosphere you only get at campsites.

The muffled murmurs of people talking in tents, children running around, the thwack of balls being kicked as dads played with young ones thrilled to be spending quality time with their parents. Couples talking quietly outside tents, sipping on cold drinks. Zips opening and closing—a sound I will always adore as it's more evocative of the summer months than anything else—all of it combined to offer a perfect backdrop to a beautiful day in a lovely location.

Mickey and Sue came over to say hi, so I made the introductions and explained to the folks that we'd met what felt like a lifetime ago at the first campsite I stayed at. The way everything had gone down there, they hadn't had the chance to meet, but were soon deep in conversation about that first murder mystery although speculation regards more recent events soon got everyone animated.

Sue, a petite young woman, in her mid-twenties like Mickey, had sun-bleached, straight blond hair, a deep tan, and was open and friendly, if rather more hesitant to speak up than her ever-jovial partner. Nevertheless, she was the first to ask, "Who did it then?"

"We don't know yet," I admitted.

"Mate, you must have some idea," chided Mickey, grinning broadly, seemingly full of unending optimism and always keen to joke around. Like Sue, he was blond, tanned, and happy, both giving off a proper surfer hippy vibe, of which they did a lot of.

"Not really. There are suspects, but there are other people to talk to."

"Like who?" asked Sue, leaning forward but keeping her hand on Mickey's knee. All he wore were cut-offs, no T-shirt, and I got the impression this was how he spent most of his time.

"The other campers, the rest of the staff at the pub. Possibly the night shift at the factory and the other people at Sunny Parks."

"What's this?" asked Mickey, eyes sparkling with mirth as though he was perpetually thinking of something funny.

Between us, we explained about what we'd been up to, and I also told about the notes in Vee. He turned from excited to serious.

"Mate, that's a real downer. You don't want things like that going down in your home. If our Dub was a crime scene, I don't know if I'd ever be able to sleep in her again."

"Our caravan had a stewed corpse in it!" declared Dad with a wave of his hands. "Look at it!"

"I know, mate. Rather you than me."

"It's just a caravan," said Mum.

"You not bothered, Jill?" asked Mickey.

"No. I'm old enough to know that it's not the dead who can hurt you."

"But the killers can," whispered Mickey, glancing around the campsite and shuddering. "These notes are a real worry. Reckon the old guy did for someone while he was pretending the van was being fixed?"

"He might have. But even the wife is suspicious. She had new carpets."

"Nothing wrong with that, mate."

"No, but it's quite soon after her husband's death, and what if it was all her, not him at all? She could tell us anything to put us off the scent. Which reminds me, I should call the garage before they close." I excused myself then made the call and got put through to the manager. After explaining who I was, which took a while, I asked if it was true that the van went in every year for a few weeks to be serviced and any issues dealt with.

He was reluctant to say, which was fair enough as he worried he was betraying a trust, I assumed, but it turned out that wasn't the case at all. He simply didn't want to talk about Noel.

They'd had a disagreement many years ago, ten he reckoned, and hadn't seen or heard from him since. Last he'd heard, from a customer, was that Noel took the van to another garage where they did same day services, just the basics, which he insisted was no way to treat an old lady like Vee.

I thanked him, hung up, and scratched my head, absentmindedly tugging at my beard as I considered things. It hadn't come as a surprise. We all had the same thought once Olive mentioned the van being gone for weeks, but now it was looking more likely than ever that Noel had been deceiving his wife, keeping the van somewhere, and possibly inside my beautiful home a desperate person had been held hostage without his wife being any the wiser.

He could have come and gone as he pleased, never

for too long, with the occasional extended stay if he skipped work or was gone under another pretence. Tomorrow, we'd have to check out the spot he frequented, although he could have taken the van anywhere.

I returned to the others and explained about the call; neither Mum nor Dad were surprised.

"He pulled a fast one on his missus," said Mickey. "He could have been doing it for years and years. A string of bodies. I bet he was back and forth to a secret location with a victim inside the van."

"Mickey, stop looking so happy," said Sue, glancing at me. "Sorry about him. He gets carried away. Ever since we met you at the first place, then again at the beach, he's been obsessed with murder."

"I have not!"

"You have. You've followed everything online about Max, and keep complaining that nobody gets murdered anywhere we stay."

"Until now. Because we've found Max, so now there are loads of bodies!" Mickey grinned as if I'd done him a massive favour.

"Stop it! Just stop it! It's horrible," wailed Sue, putting her hands to her face, her hair hanging as she bent forward, shaking.

"Sorry, love. I didn't mean to upset you. You know I'm only fooling around."

"Are you okay, dear?" asked Mum, putting her arm around Sue and pulling her in close. She shook her head and tutted at Mickey, who looked forlorn about upsetting Sue.

"I'm fine," mumbled Sue, then lifted her head, brushed back her hair, and wiped her eyes. "Thanks for the cuddle."

"Any time," beamed Mum, then released our sensitive guest.

"Love, I was only messing around," said Mickey.

"You don't normally get upset like this. What's going on?"

"I know, but it's ghastly. Gross. Who cooks someone?"

"That," said Dad, voice ominous, "is what we're going to find out!" He beamed at us, then asked, "Was that dramatic enough? I always wanted to say that."

"Awesome!" shouted Mickey, clapping his hands, then glancing at Sue and toning down his enthusiasms. "Right, we better leave you guys to it. I'm cooking tonight, so hold your noses if the wind blows the wrong way. Max, give me a shout if you need an extra pair of eyes and ears. I'd love to help out."

Taking Sue's hand, and whispering an apology to her, they returned to their VW.

"Poor girl is very delicate," said Dad. "You'd think she'd never been embroiled in a murder before."

"She hasn't. Not like we have. They were at the campsite in North Wales, and at the beach, but they weren't involved and certainly not right where it happened. This is different. But it's probably because Mickey keeps talking about it to her. Freaking her out. And let's face it. This is very gruesome."

"Then maybe vanlife isn't for her," grunted Dad. "If you're going to live in a van, you're going to encounter loads and loads of dead bodies. Some are bound to be stomach-churning."

"True," agreed Mum.

I stared at them both, waiting for them to laugh, but when they didn't I sighed and tried to explain. "Guys, what keeps happening to me is not normal. It's the opposite. Hardly anyone in the entire country gets murdered. It's a rare occurrence. No other vanlifers get caught up in this craziness. None. It's just me. At the festival, after we found the second note, it all made sense. It's not so much even me. It's Vee. The van is trying to make amends for whatever terrible thing happened in her. It's karma. Cosmic fate. Yin and yang. Balancing out the universe kind of thing. She's trying to make amends by being right at the heart of these terrible events so they can be solved and justice found for the victims. I'm a conduit of sorts, I guess. I know it sounds far-fetched, and yes, Mum, I know I sound like what you'd call a right hippy, but I'm convinced of it."

"Me too," said Mum softly with a sad smile.

"You are?"

"Yes. It makes me terribly sad, Son. I lose sleep over it. You're in so much danger. You got attacked a few weeks back, then were chasing around after killers. I worry."

"We both do."

"But you're so upbeat and unconcerned by everything," I said, nonplussed. "This hasn't fazed you in the slightest."

"That's your mother's way. You know that. She puts on a brave face. She's worried. I'm worried."

"We're both very proud of you, Max. But it's a dangerous thing you're doing." Mum dabbed at her tears with a handkerchief, then smiled. "So very proud. Me and your dad talked it through the other night, and we both came to the same conclusion as you. It's Vee. Something very bad happened and this is her way of feeling better about herself. No, that's not quite right. Vans don't have emotions, but they have energy. Hers is very positive, like yours. Like Min's. And especially Anxious'. Even like ours. We bring good vibrations to her and she appreciates it. This lump of old metal is using you to correct the balance and make everything right."

"Now who's the hippy?" I laughed, then cuddled my soppy mother as she fussed about me messing up her hair or creasing her dress even though I knew she didn't care about that.

"Hey, you two, look over there," whispered Dad, nodding his head in all directions.

"Where?" gasped Mum, eyes wide, searching the campsite.

"Don't look!" Dad hissed, wringing his hands in a

panic.

"What are you going on about, you silly man?" Mum slapped his thighs and smiled, but Dad remained looking like he'd seen a ghost.

"What's up?" I asked, surreptitiously scanning the campsite, lingering for a moment on a surprising scene then tracing back to Dad.

"You saw it, didn't you? What's he doing?"

"What is it?" asked Mum, desperate to be part of the intrigue. "I want to know too."

Dad leaned forward in his chair so we did the same until our heads almost touched, and he said, "Dan's going into that big tent that's been there all day. The old-fashioned canvas one. The ex-army model. It's pretty cool and I wonder who owns it. Think he's stealing?"

"Or hiding another body?" whispered Mum.

"He wouldn't be that brazen," I said. "But it is strange."

"He's not to be trusted." Mum's eyes widened as her imagination clearly got the better of her. "I bet he's in there plotting who the next victim will be. What if it's us?"

"I thought you weren't worried about being the next victim," teased Dad. "You said you weren't scared, and that no way it would be someone killing people from the site."

"Yes, well, that was before Dan the utterly suspicious turned up and showed his true colours."

"There's no need to get carried away," I said, trying to diffuse their growing concerns. "I'm sure there's a logical explanation."

"Then why don't you go and find out?" challenged Dad. "See what that weirdo is up to?"

"Yes, do that," agreed his partner in crime against caravans with a little too much enthusiasm.

"A moment ago, you said he was the killer. Now you want me to go over?"

"Better than us going," said Mum. "You know I'm

not good under pressure, and I'll probably say something to get him worked up then next thing you know, wham, I'm dunked in the massive pot he most likely owns and put on to simmer for dinner." Mum shuddered, then laughed nervously.

As one, we turned our heads to watch Dan exiting the tent then sitting in a fold-out chair and leaning back with an audible sigh even from across the campsite. He pulled a beer bottle from the holder in the chair's arm, took a sip, then closed his eyes.

"What's his game?" asked Dad.

"Leave this to me," I said, then stood. I whistled for Anxious who never needed much encouragement to go on an adventure, even if this was a rather brief one, and with Mum and Dad gasping dramatically, I sent Anxious off ahead over to Dan so I had an excuse to be nosy.

When I arrived, Anxious was sitting in front of Dan, wagging happily, although rather confused by the lack of attention he was receiving.

"Good boy, Anxious," I told him, then handed him half a biscuit.

My trusting pooch looked from the biscuit to me, head cocked, wondering what shenanigans I was up to by limiting his snack time like this.

"He's hungry, eh?" asked Dan as he opened his eyes and nodded.

"Yes, but he's been eating too much lately and my folks keeps giving him too many treats." I bent, then told Anxious, "Just half a biscuit. Dinner won't be too long."

He took it, settled down, and nibbled slowly, trying to prolong snack time.

"You want something?" asked Dan, eyeing me from beneath a very deep frown.

"Just wanted to say hello and let you know we visited your son earlier and had a word about the, er, incident."

"I thought I said not to interfere? Leave the police to figure this out. I don't want any trouble."

"Dan, I'm not trying to cause trouble. I'm trying to help figure out why there was a body in the caravan. I assumed you'd be pleased that someone's taken an interest. It's your business, after all."

Dan leaned forward with a scowl, and locked angry eyes on me. "You don't need to tell me that," he hissed. "I know it's my business on the line here. This is all we got, and I don't want some over-eager stranger making it even worse. Suspect my boy, do you?"

"He's a prime suspect," I admitted. "The police had been there too. You haven't heard?"

"Mike works long hours at the damn place, but at least it's a job. He's not big on sharing, especially as he's still sour about not getting what he wanted here. Not that it's any of your business, but the boy's not that quick on the uptake. He's tried various jobs here but it never works out. We would have paid him a full wage to help around the place, but he said he felt demeaned and wanted to strike out on his own. Not that he minds eating our food, paying minimal rent, and taking advantage of his mum."

"He seemed like a nice guy. Struggling a little, from what I could gather, but he's making it work at Sunny Parks."

"For now." Dan swigged his beer then lowered the bottle. Gasping, and wiping his mouth with the back of his hand, he grunted, "Boy will be back with his tail between his legs soon enough. He can't get his numbers right, and there'll be trouble, you mark my words. But that's none of your business, now is it?"

"No, not at all. Dan, I really am trying to help. I have a good track record with this kind of thing, so don't think I'm just interfering. I want to solve this. Do you have any ideas who it might have been?"

"None. Like I told the detectives, it's a real mystery." He waved it away, dismissive, which I found extremely strange considering this was his reputation on the line. "My guess is someone dumped the body before the caravan got here. Must be from Sunny Parks. Some fool panicked and put the corpse inside, then my son didn't bother checking the interior before handing it over. Dumb."

"Right, it could be that. It makes the most sense. But it still leaves the question why. Not to be nosy, although I guess I am being, but what's with the cool tent? Have you set it up for guests?"

"Nope, it's mine," he said proudly, animated for the first time, eyes bright as he studied the large army tent. "I work long hours in the restaurant, but outside is where I'm truly at home and at peace. I leave it up most of the year, and spend whatever time I can here. I sleep in this beauty most nights in the summer, and relax in the evenings if I get the chance."

"What about Joni? Does she join you?"

"Sometimes. Not often enough. She likes her comfy mattress. Anything else? Want to know the colour of my undies? How much money I owe the bank?"

I held my hands up and said, "Okay, Dan, I'll leave you to it. I meant no offence, but I can see you want to be alone."

"I do." Dan grabbed his beer and drained it, but his eyes never left mine.

I told Anxious we were leaving and he didn't even try to get a fuss from Dan. That was all the confirmation I needed that he wasn't to be trusted. Anxious knew people better than I did, and if he gave someone short shrift they were someone I had to keep an eye on.

Mum and Dad were bristling with anticipation when we returned, so I explained the situation, listened to them gossip and speculate, then continued sorting out dinner.

Chapter 8

There were times in my life when I would feel sick with stress and worry as I prepared a plate of food in a restaurant. The deeper I got into fine-dining and striving for absolute perfection with my cooking, and with my reputation growing, I became all-consumed. I neglected my personal health, my home, Anxious, and worst of all I neglected Min.

Single-minded, obsessive, determined to be the best chef in the country, I rose through the ranks quickly and was always in demand. Restaurants offered me vast sums and I was choosy once I could take my pick of where I worked. It was Michelin three-star or nothing. I knew I was good, and could pull off creating meals at the finest establishments, but running kitchens and endlessly fussing over minute details was bad for my mental health.

It took it all coming crashing down for me to finally wake up and realise that this was not what I wanted at all. That my rather obsessive nature was not a good fit for a job where even the slightest overlooked detail could see you blacklisted as a chef, making the restaurant lose their status, and for it all to fall apart.

I had an epiphany of sorts, and for the first time in my life realised that failing at work, being poor, or making mistakes was not the same as failing at life. Failing at life was actually exactly what I'd been doing by believing being a great cook was what defined me. It wasn't. Failure was letting people you loved down when you had a choice. I had one.

Forced to re-evaluate, I searched my soul and discovered that such a life wasn't what I wanted in the least. I'd simply chosen a career path and pursued it with everything I had, leaving nothing for others or myself, when it should have been the opposite.

Life wasn't about work. Life was about what made you happy. Anxious and Min made me happy.

Now I'd put that all behind me and was making amends in the best way I knew how, it had slowly dawned on me just how much I actually enjoyed cooking. It wasn't a battle of wills between me and the other chefs or the restaurant manager, or even the waiting staff. It was an almost zen-like symbiosis between me and the food. Cooking was a joy again. Simple, tasty, and fun.

It made my heart sing to put together raw ingredients and with the magic of heat turn them into something to be celebrated. How amazing! I felt like an alchemist. A true magician.

Still able to focus deeply on the cooking, I also learned how to let go and accept imperfection, and was pleased to discover it often made the end result better. More genuine. An authentic meal presented simply and with no fuss. No messing with the presentation to get it absolutely perfect, just dish it up and get to the most important part of the whole enterprise. Eating it. Relishing the flavours, savouring every mouthful. When I was working, I'd hardly have time to appreciate the taste because I was already stressing about the next dish I'd be preparing.

Which is all a very long-winded way of saying that I didn't have a heart attack when Dad insisted he be left in charge of the short rib of beef. I'd paid a fortune for it, and was going to cook on the small barbecue I'd managed to rig up with several extra grills so it could be seared off under intense heat then lifted up higher and allowed to cook slowly through until done to perfection.

The sumptuous, and so-dark-it-was-almost-black bean casserole I'd left to simmer on low was looking and tasting divine already, but I knew it needed hours before it would be perfect. With the barbecue ready to go, the smell of charcoal rich in the air, I'd covered the beef in oil and simple seasoning—no need to add anything else as the beef needed to shine through—and it was time to sear.

"Here, let me do that," offered my father casually, looking so innocent he was clearly guilty of trying to act offhand.

"No, it's okay. You both sit and relax." I paused with the tray of ribs in my hands and realised I was trembling slightly. With a wan smile, I laughed, then handed it to him and said, "You got me."

"Just checking, Son." Dad winked, then took the tray over to the barbecue.

"Old habits die hard, and I almost refused. You know it's expensive, right?" I asked, stepping closer, almost tripping over Anxious whose nose was dilating and the puddle at his feet was almost so big I'd have to change into wellies or invest in a small kayak for when it was barbecue time.

"It's just some meat, isn't it, love?" said Mum with a dastardly grin.

"Hey, stop teasing the poor lad." Dad picked up a rib with the tongs, then laid it gently on the barbecue before repeating it with the other two. "He knows we know how he always gets the best if he can. Don't worry, Max, I'm an old hand at barbecue and was doing it before you were born."

"Yes, and always burning the sausages. Maybe you should leave it to the expert?"

"Nonsense," huffed Dad, hurriedly tying the apron around his waist as the meat began to sizzle and spit. "Max trusts me, don't you?"

"Of course. But normally I do the cooking. And, er,

what will I do?"

"Obsess about if I'm doing it right? Keep a constant eye on it? Start sweating if you think I'm turning it too soon or too late?" Dad wagged a finger at me and Mum tittered, clearly happy at the banter.

"Who says? I could just close my eyes, relax, maybe have a doze. You know it needs at least an hour and a half yet, right? First you have to sear it, then you need to use those racks I've rigged up to—"

"Yes, yes, I do know how to cook this," sighed Dad. "I've got a better idea. There's no point us sitting and watching you get antsy, so give it five while I sear it, and yes, I'll do the sides, too, then we can do something."

"Like what?" asked Mum, always suspicious when Dad had one of his "brilliant ideas" without her suggesting it first.

"You'll see."

To distract myself, I checked on the mixed bean stew, added a squeeze of tomato paste, a pinch of Maldon sea salt, a quick dash of brown sauce, then stirred before turning the heat down as low as it would go and feeling better about knowing it would be perfect. At the very end, I'd add a handful of chopped parsley and coriander and it would be divine with the meat. Assuming, of course, that Dad fulfilled his promise and didn't incinerate it.

Trying my best to relax, knowing it didn't matter and that the company was more important, I poured us all a glass of wine.

"Thought we were going to go and visit the spot where Noel and Olive used to take the campervan?" asked Mum. "You aren't going to drink and drive, are you? Don't forget, you had a little glass earlier."

"Of course not. If it's alright with you guys, I think it's better to go in the morning. Otherwise, we'll be rushing, and I want to take my time looking around. And besides, I'm sure we'll be too full to move after our dinner."

"Oh, hooray," squealed Mum. "I'm absolutely

shattered and could sit here for the rest of the day. A drink sounds lovely. Cheers."

Dad left the barbecue and took a glass, then we clinked and drank.

After a long, hot, stressful, and extremely peculiar day, the Cava went down a treat.

Smoke filled the air as we sat around chatting and laughing while Dad kept an eye on the barbecue and I tried to ignore it completely. Anxious made sure to watch over things, though, willing the delicious smelling beef to leap from the grill into his salivating maw.

After Dad flipped the beef carefully and I hid my eyes behind my hands, much to Mum's amusement, he retreated to the car then returned with a football.

"Fancy a game?"

"Wow! We haven't played in years. Sure, that would be great. Mum, are you playing?"

"Of course I am. I've even got my trainers on."

"When we were packing, I found it in the garage and it brought back so many memories. We used to play all the time in the garden or at the park. So long ago now," said Dad, a faraway look in his eyes, "but we can't be that rusty."

"I used to love it when we went to the park on a Sunday afternoon, then came home tired and dirty. We'd rush into the kitchen to get a whiff of Mum's Sunday dinner. It was always the best, Mum. Better than the Bisto advert."

"You boys were always pestering me for a taste of the meat, then complaining when I told you to go and wash up."

"You always looked after us," said Dad with a wink. "Still do."

"Don't you ever forget it." Mum smiled happily, eyes unfocused as she recalled the past.

For the next half an hour, it was like the years had never passed and I was a child again. Hanging with my parents, kicking a ball around, the smell of meat cooking. Recapturing it just for a brief reminder of when life was more innocent and carefree, all worries put aside, was one of the most special moments I ever had with my parents.

Dad was still a fine footballer, running rings around us, his ball skills something I'd never been able to match. But we both tried, and teamed up to get a few goals between the sticks I'd set up to act as goalposts.

Finally, exhausted, sweaty, but laughing, we returned to the barbecue and stood around it, taking in the divine smells and congratulating Dad on a job well done.

"Still a good while to go," he said, carefully inspecting the meat, "but it'll be worth the wait."

And oh boy, was it ever.

"Dad, and it pains me to say this, that was the best beef short rib I have ever tasted. Dark, almost burned on the outside, the fat was rendered down, and perfectly pink on the inside. It was so soft it just melted."

"You did an impressive job, love."

"Thank you." Dad took a bow, but from a seated position as none of us could move. "Told you I would nail it."

"And you did. Sorry for being awkward about it earlier."

"Max, it's okay. After all, this was your treat, so of course you wanted to cook it. We know you enjoy spoiling us. But sometimes it's good to let go, take a step back, and let others show you that they're capable too."

"You're right, and thanks. So, what's for dinner tomorrow?"

Dad blanched. "That's my cooking done for the year. You know your mother doesn't let me near the kitchen."

"Only because you never offer, and I value my health. If it was down to you, it would be pie and chips every night."

"Nothing wrong with pie and chips," laughed Dad,

winking at me.

Anxious kept a keen eye on everyone while we sat with our plates in our laps, but he was sorely disappointed to find that not only had everyone eaten all they were given, but the leftovers weren't automatically dropped into his now empty bowl. He'd already had more than he should have, so I finally heaved to my feet and wrapped up the remaining beef in foil then placed it into Tupperware and popped the container in the fridge. Stepping up into Vee felt like scaling Everest, but I managed it with the help of crampons and rope, although I did get a stitch.

I insisted that my folks relax while I happily pottered about cleaning everything and storing the remaining stew, which was amazing and elicited numerous murmurs of approval, but there was no doubt Dad had done himself, and the beef, proud.

After everything was washed, I ran a brush over the barbecue and grill, partly because I knew I'd forget if I didn't do it right away, and partly because I could guarantee that Anxious would burn his tongue as he tried to get the crusty bits.

With everything washed and dried, I turned my attention to the kitchen and stacked everything away in the best order to make life easy next time, then sealed the lids, gave the counter a spray and wipe down, then stood back and grunted in satisfaction.

"Will you look at him?" laughed Mum.

"He's always been the same. Even as a lad."

"What are you two talking about?"

"You always liked things just so. When your mum cooked, you used to beg to be allowed to wipe the counters and do the drying up. Every other child on the planet would moan and try to get out of it, but not you."

"He was a good boy. That's his way. It wasn't about cleaning, though, it was about the kitchen. You adored being in there. You were my little helper."

"I don't remember too much about that," I confessed.

"But I do know we used to have fun."

"We did. I loved having you there with me. There was something about the kitchen that was in your bones. You've always been the same. And it's nice to see that you still stay organised."

"Don't know where he gets that from," grunted Dad.

"I'm organised!"

"Mum, you're a nightmare. You leave things everywhere and never tidy up after yourself."

"But I clean the house every day," she protested.

"Yes, but half of that time is spent picking up stuff you've dropped, or things you lost because you never put them in the right place to begin with," teased Dad.

"You're a fine one to talk," grumbled Mum. She smiled and added, "My boys. I love you both so much."

"And we love you!" we chorused.

"You daft lumps," she chuckled, beaming from ear to ear.

Anxious yipped because our excitement had caused him to believe something utterly awesome was happening, so, of course, that meant a walk.

Although we could have all happily remained exactly where we were, we agreed that a stroll would do us good and help burn off some of the calories, so we locked up, understandably nervous after recent events, then wandered through the campsite, nodding to people, saying hello, but not getting involved in too much conversation. It felt odd, because people were wary and hardly spoke, when I'd expected everyone to be falling over themselves to ask about the murder.

Most had now spoken to the police either in person or on the phone, but there was a distinct lack of interest in what, after all, had been a very grisly discovery.

"They're acting weird," noted Mum as we crossed the road from the restaurant and slipped through a gate onto a footpath that cut across an open field.

"They're probably too afraid to speak to the maniacs with the bright pink caravan," teased Dad.

"It's lovely. And normally people want the gossip. Maybe they don't know."

"They must do. Most weren't there when you arrived, but the police were back again, remember, and spoke to a lot of them. I think it's nerves, and them not being sure about us. Or maybe they're all in on it and they were planning on having a campsite feast." Dad sniggered, but was soon cut off.

"Stop it, you utter pilchard," warned Mum.

"I am not a pilchard. That's my saying and you stole it. You're the pilchard."

"Pilchard," countered Mum, her tone ensuring we understood her word was final.

Anxious ran circles around us, joyous to be out in the open and able to stretch his legs properly, so I didn't even need the ball flinger. We circled the field slowly, everyone exhausted after the long, peculiar day, and laughed at the little guy as he barked at birds that flocked together and took delight in teasing him by swooping low and flying just ahead as he pelted through the long grass, almost lost to sight.

Once he was thoroughly exhausted and walking by our side, we returned to the campsite and relaxed with a cool glass of wine in hand. The two keen additions to team "amateur detectives" took turns unloading the car and organising the caravan, not a word said about it being weird.

As dusk morphed to full night, I turned on a few solar lights I'd had charging. It was cosy, and dreamlike as we listened to the birds settle and the other campers slowly retire or relax with drinks while children protested about brushing their teeth and why couldn't they stay up later.

Finally, it was time for bed. I groaned as I'd forgotten to pull out the Rock n Roll bed yet again, something I'd become almost religious about doing immediately after dinner now, so sorted that then returned to find my parents standing outside the caravan for crazies, fidgeting and shifting from foot to foot.

"What's up?"

"Can we sleep with you tonight?" blurted Mum.

"I thought you were okay with what happened in there?"

"I was, but now it's bedtime I'm feeling weird about it. Maybe just for tonight until I get used to it. It's not for me. It's your dad. He's a big baby."

"I told you, I can sleep in there no problem!" Dad cast a worried glance at the caravan and shuddered.

"There's not really room for three. You take Vee, and I'll use the caravan."

"No, Son, we can't let you do that," protested Dad.

"It's fine, honestly. I don't mind. I've been around so much weirdness lately that I'll be out like a light. Don't worry about it."

"Are you sure?" asked Mum. "We don't want to put you out. It's your home, after all."

"Of course it's alright. You get settled and have a nice sleep. I'll take the caravan, and tomorrow we can swap back. On one condition."

"Yes?" asked Mum warily.

"You don't mess up my systems. Don't empty the drawers, don't leave your stuff everywhere, and do not get make-up on the bed."

"I never do."

"You do," said Dad.

"Last time you stayed, I had to wash the sheets twice before it came out. So remove it before you get into bed."

"All of it?" Mum jumped back, aghast. "What if I have to get up in the night and go outside? Someone might see."

"Why would you have to do that? And it'll be dark."

"There might be a fire, or an emergency."

"And why would anyone care if you had your make-up on or not?" I asked.

"You know I always wear my face. It's who I am."

"Then seeing as we're being more relaxed about what we obsess over, why not do things differently tonight?" I asked, trying not to smile.

"He's got you there, love. If Max can let me cook his posh beef, you can remove your make-up. It's only me in there, and I've seen you without it before. Come on, it's getting late, and I'm done for."

"Fine, but if there's a fire it's your fault if I scare people when they see me without my eyeliner," warned Mum.

"I'll take my chances," I chuckled.

We said goodnight, and with a little trepidation Anxious and I entered the pink hellhole.

Chapter 9

"It's okay. Try to rest," I whispered into Anxious' twitching ear as he sat beside me on the bed, trembling as he glanced away to the door.

Neither of us had managed to settle, and at two I'd finally accepted we needed a light on so he would calm down. I needed it too. The mind is a funny thing and plays all kinds of tricks on you in the small hours. Ours had been running on overdrive ever since we got tucked in under the blankets so only our heads were visible, and lay back on the pillows.

Although I knew the door was locked and nobody was about to come and stew us, I imagined endless awful things happening, and Anxious was clearly having the same issues. His tiny body trembled, causing the bed frame to squeak and my stress levels to escalate.

Utterly stupid on my part, as I was a large guy with an independent mind and had no qualms about defending myself. I'd never been unduly concerned for my safety before, but there was something about this case, and the macabre circumstances, that rankled. It was the stupid caravan. That was the real issue.

With the light on, pink shade of course, the room was cast in a sickly sweet pastel hue that reminded me of watered down blood. It was downright eerie, bordering on psychotic. What kind of utter maniac designed this monstrosity? Strange shadows danced with every shake of Anxious' body, flickering monsters cavorting across the walls. Peculiar creaks of the caravan settling caused my best buddy to sit bolt upright and whimper.

When the kettle inexplicably flicked on and steam billowed into the bedroom, in my half comatose state I jumped up in an utter panic, believing the killer was trying to steam us where we lay.

"That's it! Come on, let's make a cuppa and go outside. Neither of us are going to sleep in here. It's a perversion of all that's great about this life."

Anxious rocketed off the bed, tail wagging, so I opened the door and let him out before making myself a milky tea with two sugars—not my usual style—then took it outside and sank into my chair. Relief washed over me as I eyed the caravan dubiously and vowed never to set foot inside such a blasphemous crime against road travel ever again.

The sound of my parents snoring from my beloved VW was strangely comforting, and when Anxious' peaceful grunts joined them I smiled as I spied him under Vee, happily sleeping now he was close to his home again and where he felt safe from the monsters lurking in pink shadows.

After my tea, I hunkered down low and finally drifted off.

Steam clouded my vision as I opened my eyes, and I panicked, thinking I was back in the caravan and being cooked.

"Tea, love?" asked Mum with a sympathetic smile as she waved the mug in front of my face.

"Oh, wow, I thought I was being cooked alive." I rubbed my face and shifted in the chair, my back creaking.

"It's just tea. What are you doing out here? Fancied an early morning then dozed back off?"

"Something like that," I mumbled, taking the tea

gratefully.

"The poor lad's probably been out here most of the night," said Dad with sympathy as he rolled up his white T-shirt sleeves, completing the Teddy Boy look he adored.

"Don't be such a numpty." Mum glared at him, but he was busy putting his steel comb through his Brylcreemed hair so avoided retina burn.

"Told you we shouldn't have taken his campervan," gloated Dad.

"You haven't been out here all night, have you?" Mum frowned and tugged at her red and white bandanna nervously.

"No, of course not! Just got up early then fell back to sleep. What time is it?"

"Almost nine." Dad caught my eye and nodded; his way of saying thank you for not upsetting Mum but that he knew the truth.

"You needed the rest," cooed Mum, back in fuss-mode. "We all had a wonderful sleep then! That was an exciting day yesterday, but today will be even better."

"Better? Are you mad, woman? We got a bright pink caravan, there was a stewed guy inside, we went chasing all over, Max is wiped out, and Anxious won't come out from under Vee."

"He's just sleepy," said Mum happily, oblivious. "I'm making scrambled eggs on toast, so you boys relax."

I suddenly felt very chilly and shuddered. Cautiously, I asked, "Have you started?" not wanting to look at my kitchen for fear of what I might find.

"Oh, she's started all right," warned Dad. "Been at it for ages. You might want to visit the bathroom and keep your head turned the other way. I'll sort out the kitchen once we finish eating."

The temptation was almost too much to resist, but I followed his advice, got a few things from Vee, wincing at the carnage inside as Mum had spread her make-up and clothes over every available surface and even made new ones by stacking books and trays on top of her stuff to create more room, then headed to the facilities without even glancing at my lovely, well-organised outdoor kitchen.

On my return, I bumped into Joni.

"Hi."

"Oh, hi, Max. Gosh, you don't look like you had the best night's sleep."

"I swapped with my folks, so had the caravan."

"Enough said." She smiled sympathetically and fidgeted with her curls for a moment before blurting, "Max, you will help figure this out, won't you? I read about you last night, and you have an incredible knack for solving mysteries. My Dan said he warned you off, told you not to interfere again, but please don't listen to him. This has me terrified. About everyone's safety, about the business, about everything. Please help us."

"Don't worry, I'll do what I can. We have a trip planned for today, but I haven't forgotten about this. How could I?"

"You mean it? The police called this morning and are coming over to talk to the last of the guests, which I could do without, but at least they might uncover something. I've already spoken to everyone, but nobody seems suspicious. It's just families or hikers, and that lovely couple Mickey and Sue."

"I haven't spoken to everyone here yet, as they're giving me a wide berth, but I promise I will today. Try not to worry. What are you up to now? Just checking on things?"

"I need to wake Dan up. He sleeps in the tent a lot, and he's overslept again." Joni's eye twitched as she tried to hide a scowl, but it was clearly a bone of contention.

"Problems?"

Joni shrugged. "The usual marital strife. I wish he'd stop dreaming things could be different. We do okay here and it's a business and income, but he's never happy.

Always wants more, you know? Sometimes you need to be content with your lot and appreciate what you have, not chase after things that will never make you happy."

"Joni, you're a wise woman. And hang in there. You never know, the detectives might have some information today."

"I hope so. This is beyond stressful. Come for dinner this evening at the restaurant. It's on me."

"No, I wouldn't dream of it. Maybe we will come, but we'll pay."

"I honestly want it to be my treat. Don't worry about what Dan says."

"It isn't that. It's a thing I have. I prefer to pay my own way. But we'll see you later."

Joni nodded then hurried over to Dan's tent.

Knowing Mum would be some time even though it was a simple breakfast of eggs and toast, I did the rounds of the campsite, and managed to speak to everyone I hadn't had a chance to talk to, or others I'd got to know a little before yesterday's incident.

I bypassed the elderly couple who'd hardly moved since their arrival, having heard in rather too much detail about dodgy hips and bad knees. It wasn't because they weren't lovely people, they were, and the lady made the best tea I'd ever drunk, but because I was confident they weren't the guilty party.

The young couple with two raucous children were the same. No way it could have been them. The energetic youngsters ran around from morning to night, seemingly unstoppable, and they were frazzled enough without me interfering.

Mickey and Sue waved and smiled happily as they pottered about under their sun shelter, sorting their own outdoor kitchen in-between kissing and hugging. They were so kind and friendly, and it was nice to think that there were similar people travelling around the country and we would bump into each other every so often. It made it feel like a real family.

I spied the lone hiker who had been here for a few days. He was a quiet man, but got rather excited when conversation turned to the routes he was exploring, but there was definitely something off about him. I wandered over to say hello, just to get more of a feel for this short, stout guy who never moved without his face buried in a plastic-coated map.

"Hi, John. Another beautiful day in paradise." I waved as I approached, not wanting to startle this nervous man.

"Max, are you only just getting ready for the day?"

"Yes. It wasn't the best of nights."

"No, I can imagine. Um, sorry about the corpse in the caravan," he mumbled, fiddling with his green sun hat then tugging at his khaki waistcoat with just about all the pockets.

"Yes, it was a big shock. You spoke to the detectives, didn't you?"

"I did. Gosh, that was very worrying. I was so nervous. I felt guilty even though I hadn't done anything wrong. They make you feel that way on purpose," he confided, moving in close, his missing incisor drawing my eyes to the gap and his thick, dry lips.

"The authorities often make you feel like that," I agreed. "I know we haven't spoken since it happened, and I understand your reticence to come over, but is there anything you saw or heard that might help?"

"Nothing, I swear." He wiped his forehead and glanced around as though about to be arrested.

"Hey, it's okay. I'm not accusing you. I just wondered. No new people, or anything untoward?"

"There was that fellow who left the day before yesterday. He wasn't a hiker, just sat around drinking beer and tapping his phone for a day then packed up. I think he might have been having marital issues. Apart from him, nothing. No new arrivals since your parents. They settling in okay?" John's hand shot to his mouth and his colour rose. "Sorry, sorry. Dumb question. They had a body in their caravan. Um, Max?"

"Yes?"

"Why is it pink? It's very bright, and doesn't really go with a quiet campsite. Not that I mind. It's just…"

"Very, very pink," I laughed.

"Yes."

"It's a good question, and one only my mother can answer. She likes it, so what can you do?"

"I suppose. And what happened? The detectives didn't give many details, only that a body was found. What was it like?" John's eyes bored into mine, as though he wanted a picture of the corpse, and he licked his lips.

"Not nice. Let's leave it at that. So, you going hiking today?"

"Oh yes, every day. I have the route planned out, with a nice stop off for lunch at a pub, then I'll be back this evening for dinner in the restaurant."

"Sounds like a good plan. Have a great day." I waved, then left before John began regaling me with every detail of his route.

Back at the campervan, I kept my head down, sat in my chair facing away from the kitchen, and tried not to wince at the worrying sounds coming from behind me as Mum prepared breakfast.

Anxious came and said good morning, and Dad joined me and explained that they'd already been for a walk, so I could relax. We sat and chatted while Mum clattered around and muttered about it being like cooking for cavemen, which was rather harsh.

The new chef in town beamed as she placed a massive bowl of scrambled eggs on the tiny green table, followed up by a teetering tower of toast. "Here we go!"

"Did you use the whole loaf?" asked Dad.

"Of course! We need our energy for a busy day. And

you're both growing boys."

"I'm in my thirties, Dad's in his fifties. Hardly boys."

"Maybe not, but someone's still growing." Mum slapped Dad's tummy and guffawed.

"It's still perfectly flat," he complained. "I look after myself."

"I know that, love. I was only teasing. You look very fit and nowhere near your age." Mum winked at me as the love of her life, besides me of course!, beamed with pride.

"Tuck in then. I splashed Tabasco in the scrambled eggs and I did them nice and soft how you both like them. I also used your posh Maldon sea salt and some black pepper."

"Looks awesome," I said, my stomach rumbling.

Anxious whined from beside Mum; he loved her scrambled eggs but didn't get to sample them very often.

"Silly boy. As if I could forget about you!"

Anxious wagged joyously and rubbed against Mum's legs as she returned to the kitchen and retrieved a small bowl for the starving pooch. Once he was happily eating, then finished, as eggs go down easily, she joined us and we tucked in.

Silence reigned supreme while we ate, just a few murmurs of contentment and telling Mum how great they were, which made her smile the whole way through breakfast.

"That was lovely, Mum. Thank you."

"My pleasure, love. What with Jack cooking last night, and you doing the bean stew, and me never getting a look in, I wanted to at least make breakfast."

"And very fine it was, too, love. Good job." Dad leaned over and kissed her cheek then added, "Don't forget. No looking." With a wink, he took my plate, then cleaned up the rest and began the no doubt arduous job of sorting out the kitchen.

Mum retreated into the campervan to sort a few

things out, which most likely meant more mess, so I was shocked to see her exit ten minutes later with several bags.

"What are you doing?"

"I don't like it in there. It's too small and the bed's weird. It's not full-size. We'll sleep in the caravan tonight."

"Are you sure? You aren't freaked out by it now?"

"Don't be daft." Mum waved it away as nonsense. "I got the jitters yesterday, but I'm fine now. And you don't fool me, Max Effort. I know you and Anxious were scared and didn't sleep a wink. Leave it to your old mum to protect her favourite boys."

Anxious barked for joy and followed up with a howl, then launched into Vee; when I heard a creak, I knew he'd got onto the bed. He missed our home as much as me.

"I honestly don't mind. I did get carried away last night, but I'll be fine tonight. You can stay in Vee."

"Max, if it's all the same with you, I'd rather not. It's like sleeping in your bedroom and it feels weird. I prefer the caravan. We'll be fine. And anyway, I want to enjoy the pink loveliness." Mum sang to herself quietly as she began the arduous task of moving homes. I helped out with bags, but then she shooed me away, concerned I'd uncover her secret clothes. Whatever that meant. I dared not ask for fear of getting an answer. My parents were adventurous sorts, so some things were best left between man and wife, definitely not getting the son involved.

An hour later, and with the morning already half over, we were finally ready to go.

"Wow, Mum, you look even more fancy than usual!"

"Thanks, love. You know I like to make an effort."

"We made an Effort alright," chortled Dad. "I remember that afternoon very well."

"Stop," hissed Mum, glancing at me.

"Afternoon?" I asked.

"Yeah, your mother and I were on a walk in the woods. It was a warm afternoon, and we were feeling frisky so—"

"Lalala. Can't hear you!" I shouted, my fingers in my ears. When Dad stopped talking, I removed my fingers and ordered, "Never speak of such things again. I do not, ever, ever, want to know about my conception."

"Hey, there's nothing to be embarrassed about. Every single person on the planet is only here because their parents had sex."

"Exactly, and every single child on the planet does not want to think about it."

"What about IVF?" asked Mum.

"What about it?" asked Dad, confused.

"Those children weren't born through intercourse."

"Stop saying intercourse!" I wailed.

"No, maybe not," continued Dad like I hadn't spoken, "but a woman had to supply her eggs, and some guy still had to go to a clinic, get a test-tube, and—"

"No, absolutely not!" I warned. "Let's just go."

"It was a lovely day, though," sighed Mum, pinching Dad's bum.

I couldn't start Vee fast enough. Anxious rode up front with me this time, while the two lovebirds cuddled in the back.

Chapter 10

Sunlight dazzled, traffic was light, Mum and Dad giggled like excited children, Anxious kept smiling, my mixtape played some incredible eighties tracks, and the scenery was stunning, yet I couldn't shake a feeling of impending doom.

Every time I glanced at the directions on my phone propped up beside me, I could picture the messages I'd photographed. The first read HELP ME, the second was a longer note on modern lined paper saying the author had been trapped in Vee for weeks.

What did it really mean? I'd gone over and over it so many times in my head, but couldn't reconcile the messages with an answer that made sense. If Noel, the previous owner, did take the campervan away for weeks at a time but pretended it was in the garage, then how on earth did he keep someone held hostage inside?

You could easily escape unless you were tied up, and if you were shackled how would you survive? What if someone stumbled across the campervan while Noel wasn't there? If you were truly unable to move around the small space, then how did you eat and drink or go to the toilet? How could the victims have written the notes if they were incapacitated? How could they hide one under the bed where it might have never been found, or behind the panel in the cupboard?

Nothing added up, nothing made sense, and nothing had turned up, until now, that might shed some light on this most puzzling conundrum.

At least we now had something to go on. Noel had lied about the yearly service, and we were closing in on the spot he and his wife liked to frequent, and where he'd come for a day or two away alone, but there was absolutely nothing else that I could think of to do.

Rolling hills shone golden as wheat rippled with a passing breeze, almost blinding. The road shimmered as the surface temperature increased so much there had been numerous reports of the tarmac actually melting. The grass was so dry it had lost much of its colour, unheard of in this green and pleasant land, and there were now hosepipe bans throughout the country as reservoirs got worryingly low.

Yet it was truly spectacular. Under a bright blue sky, the world was alive like at no other time I could remember. But my spirits were low as we closed in on the location and even the lovebirds in the back had gone quiet, the dark mood pervasive.

Off the main road, we drove through country lanes for ten minutes, then I took a turn onto little more than a dirt track with a wondrous forest either side full of ancient oaks and stupendous beech reaching for the sun. A pristine, and rare, slice of the British countryside as it would have been thousands of years ago before most trees were cut down and land cleared to make way for agriculture and the ever-increasing demands of the burgeoning population.

It was a real beauty spot, yet clearly not known by many as there were no markers for paths or anything apart from unspoilt nature.

I checked the directions then followed the faint track until I came to a natural clearing where the grass was short and parched, then pulled on the handbrake, put Vee into neutral, and turned off the engine.

Anxious tore off once I opened the door and told

him he could go and explore. He barked excitedly as he dashed this way and that, tracking scents of rabbits or possibly even deer.

"What an amazing place," gasped Dad.

"It's special," whispered Mum. "Almost magical."

"It is. It's not just me, is it? You can feel something different here, can't you?"

"You get areas like this sometimes," said Dad as he smiled. "Special places where everything is somehow just better. It's rare, and often you don't even know what it is that makes it stand out, but you feel it in your bones. Makes you happy, doesn't it?"

"It does!" gushed Mum, grinning at Dad, then me, before wandering off in a daze.

Us guys were rooted to the spot, smiling at each other as though we'd won a million on the lottery.

"Can you smell that?" I asked, finally coming back to myself.

"It's like all the flowers rolled up into a beautiful smelling ball of loveliness."

"Weird, right? All I see is grass and trees." A breeze tickled my face, cooling the sweat, before it was gone, leaving me panting and utterly confused. "What's going on here? It's so humid, and yet I don't care."

"It's a real micro-climate." Dad shook out his legs like he'd forgotten how they worked, then sniffed loudly. "There's definitely something in the air. And the birds are louder, and I hear loads of bees. I can see why they loved coming here."

"Me too. But let's not forget why we came."

My words broke the spell and our smiles faded, replaced with a determination to uncover the truth.

"Let's get to it then," grunted Dad as he nodded.

"First thing to do is wander around and discover exactly where Noel parked the camper. Everywhere here is perfect, but he must have kept the van hidden or anyone could have found it."

"Assuming he even brought it here. We might be on a total wild goose chase."

"Maybe, but I don't think so."

"Got one of your feelings, eh?" asked Dad, his good mood returning as he winked then slapped me on the back.

"Yes. I know this is it. This is where he came with the van."

"Then let's solve this case, Max. It's been bugging me no end. What with this and the problem back at the campsite, I'm amazed I'm not a bag of nerves."

"We'll figure it out, don't you worry." I truly felt like something had changed. I didn't know why, but I was convinced we were in the right place and that finally I'd get some answers.

Still light-headed because of the peculiar atmosphere, when I turned back to Vee it was almost as though she smiled. Maybe because of the way the sunlight hit the chrome, or a shadow cast by a bird passing overhead, I wasn't sure, but studying my home it was as though she was settled. Like she knew this place, yet didn't seem sad. Rather, it was the opposite. As though pleasant times were had here and the memories had seeped into the fabric of the grass and trees.

Olive and Noel must have enjoyed numerous happy trips here over the years, but hadn't been for some time according to Olive. Why was that? Just Noel coming now and then on his own? What happened here? I had to find out.

The clearing was large enough to turn Vee around in, the short grass clearly grazed by the local deer as there was no sign of sheep. Trees cast welcome shade so I hurried over to the cooler section and slowly came back to myself. The forest was light and airy, the large specimens hogging the light so it wasn't packed with saplings, but there was a pleasant mix of new and old. Nature doing what it did best and finding a way to thrive in this oasis surrounded by farmland.

With no sign of anyone ever having been here, I found it perplexing. Were Vee's previous owners merely good vanlifers and ensured they never left anything behind when they drove off, or was this the wrong spot? I checked my phone again to confirm, and couldn't resist studying the photo of the message. With a shiver, I pocketed my Motorola and let the energy of this place sink into my bones.

Smiling as I watched my parents wandering around whilst holding hands, I cleared my mind and took in every detail I could. Something would catch my eye, or I would get inspired, because I knew I was good at this, and had finally accepted that solving mysteries wasn't something I had to be bashful about. Cautious, never over-confident, but I was able to uncover things nobody else could, so why try to deny it?

When nothing presented itself, I toured the perimeter carefully, senses alert, but never focusing on any one thing for too long. The others left me to it, knowing I needed to concentrate, and even Anxious had vanished into the trees.

At the far end, I stopped when I felt the ground become harder, and bent to find that the grass was struggling to grow and was paler. Signs of a disturbance. Ash and small coals proved someone had used this spot some time ago to have a fire, most likely in a small brazier or something similar. Keeping low, I swept my hands over the earth in case there was anything hidden, and came up with what appeared to be the back of a silver earring.

The ground was uneven in places, small divots where chairs may have been placed, the legs sinking into the ground when it wasn't as dry. This was the spot either Noel, or he and his wife, had used on multiple occasions.

The trees had been pruned back a little, creating open ground below low-hanging branches that afforded some shelter from the weather, so it was the perfect spot. But it wasn't hidden away. It was in plain sight. How could you keep someone captive here?

Standing, I moved into the trees to investigate, but there was nothing of interest. I returned to the clearing to find Anxious with my folks, tail swishing happily as they fussed over him with high-pitched voices and spoke like he was a small child. Anxious reared up on his hind legs and rested his paws on Dad as he bent to give him a treat.

"I saw that! I thought we'd agreed to go easy on the biscuits? He needs to stay trim."

"There's nothing of the little guy," said Dad with a guilty look. "And he's such a good boy."

Anxious wagged with excitement, then dashed over to Vee to snaffle his snack before anyone changed their minds, and I couldn't help smiling.

"What have you found?" asked Mum.

"Just the remains of a fire and the back of an earring. It might be Olive's, and I suppose I shouldn't have touched it, but I took a photo of where it was just in case it's evidence."

"A thing like that could be anyone's," said Dad.

"True. But I get the impression that nobody ever comes here. The way in was almost overgrown, and I doubt anyone's been since Noel. I wonder how they found it in the first place?"

"It's a real treasure of a spot," gushed Mum. "I love it. We didn't find any clues, but you're the expert. Have you finished looking?"

"Not yet, no. And don't forget that Dad was the one who helped find the clues on our first ever mystery."

"I did," he beamed, puffing out his chest. "But nothing today, Son. Sorry."

"That's okay. Can we keep looking? There has to be something here. If Noel held someone captive, there must be a sign of it somewhere. I don't know what to think about this place, as it feels so nice, a truly happy vibe, but this is where he came, and there's nothing else to go on, so let's not give up yet."

With a nod, we split up again and continued to search, but it really was just a clearing in the woods with nothing apart from a few coals and part of an earring to signify anyone's presence.

After another fruitless search, I sighed as I joined Anxious who was sitting and staring intently at a tree.

"He's been doing that for ten minutes now," noted Dad.

"Daft lump is suspicious of trees." Mum shook her head and tutted at me.

"You can't blame me for that!" I said, crouching beside my focused dog.

"You've made him too suspicious of everything. This skullduggery has messed with his head. He'll be suspecting the grass of crimes next," warned Mum with another tut.

"What is it, boy? What's with the tree?"

Anxious looked from the tree to me then back again before standing, barking, and trotting towards it. But rather than stop, he continued into the woods, before turning and wagging.

"He wants us to follow," I said.

"Oh, maybe he's finally found something." Mum rubbed her hands together and grabbed Dad, then hurried after him, speedy because she had the right footwear on for a change.

I followed behind, noting the route Anxious took, realising that this was a path of sorts, albeit a natural one that skirted the trees. The ground was worn here, subtle, but it was there, and the further we got into the woods, the faster my heart beat.

After five minutes of slow walking heading east in a mostly straight line, we stopped when we reached the edge of the forest. Before us lay hills dotted with sheep like little fluffy clouds as the sun bounced off their backs. Fields of crops in a patchwork of browns, yellows, and greens were more stunning than any painting, and the scent of flowers that entranced us earlier was almost overpowering now.

"Where's that smell coming from?" asked Dad.

Again, Anxious was the one to answer as he yipped then trotted off along the treeline.

We followed, and within minutes had dropped down the rise. We gasped at the scene before us. A large garden brimming with flowers of every description. Bright reds and yellows dominated, but with a healthy mix of purples from verbena, their high, clustered heads appearing to float above the densely packed garden as they swayed gently.

Hidden by the land rising, and yet open to the fields of grazing sheep, the property had stunning views and the forest as a backdrop. A truly beautiful location. A long cottage with a high-pitched roof clad in red tile, blue painted windows and doors, and constructed from local stone hunkered down as if embarrassed by the majesty that surrounded it. Roses rambled all over the building, almost swamping it.

"Now we know where the smell was coming from," said Dad as he snorted. "Ah, lovely. Wonder who lives here?"

Anxious barked as a gate I hadn't even noticed suddenly opened and a lady appeared.

"Can I help you?" she asked, not unfriendly, but hardly inviting us in for tea either.

"Sorry to disturb you. We didn't know there was a house here," I said. "It's so well hidden."

"From some directions, but as you can see, I'm actually rather exposed here."

"Your vest is rather low-cut, yes," trilled Mum happily.

"I meant the property," said the owner with a frown of confusion before glancing down at her simple white vest.

"Stop staring," I warned Dad with a nudge.

"I wasn't. Is this your gaff then?" he asked, extending his hand. "I'm Jack, this is my wife, Jill, that's our son, Max, and the little guy is Anxious."

"Oh, the poor thing. Has something happened?"

Anxious barked happily and sat in front of the owner, tail wagging as he waited to be adored.

"It's his name, not his emotional state," I explained for the thousandth time.

"Oh, yes, I get it. Very funny. I'm Constance," she said, chuckling.

We all shook hands then she bent and made a fuss of my patient dog, who took to her instantly.

Constance was in her early sixties with a trim body from her gardening, with no make-up, rather unkempt hair hanging low under a battered straw hat, and a deep tan. With a ready smile and a firm grip, I took to her as quickly as Anxious.

"Have you lived here long?" asked Mum.

"A few years now, but not long really. I think I've spent every waking hour the last two years out in the garden, so I'm afraid the house is still rather musty and in need of a do-over. But who has the time when there's so much to do outside?"

"We could smell the flowers from the other side of the woods, but didn't know where it was coming from," I explained. "Anxious here found a little path, so we followed him. We didn't mean to intrude."

"Don't be silly. You aren't intruding, and I don't own the countryside. Would you like to see the garden? I don't get many visitors out here, and it's just me, so company is always welcome."

We nodded to each other then said it would be lovely, so Constance led us through the gate and into her little slice of paradise.

"Blimey! You weren't joking about this taking up all

your time," said Dad as we paused inside the gate and took in the full majesty of the garden.

At least half an acre, it was a series of winding paths and seating areas with just a small patch of lawn where a blanket was laid out with a book on a side table where a jug of something cold and wet sweated through the heat.

"I was reading not long ago, with a nice frosty glass of lemonade, but then I got antsy and started weeding. I'm afraid I can't sit still for long." Constance laughed, her head flung back, eyes sparkling with mirth. The outdoors life clearly suited her.

"It's good to keep busy," agreed Dad.

"Now," she mused, hands on hips, "which one shall I murder first?"

Chapter 11

Anxious's tail swished as he studied Constance with adoring eyes. The rest of us jumped back, panicked, while I wondered how I'd got things so very, very wrong.

Constance frowned as she waved her pruning clippers around and said, "The weeds. They're poking through the path, see?" She pointed at the dandelions at our feet in the gravel as her eyes widened and she laughed. "You thought I meant you, didn't you? How funny."

"I didn't!" huffed Dad, relaxing his grip on my shoulder.

"Liar," I said, beyond relieved.

"We're involved in a murder mystery, so we have it on the brain," admitted Mum, stepping out from behind Dad.

"Really? How exciting. Is it gruesome? What happened?"

Once we'd explained about the campsite killing, which Constance was very interested in, she showed us around the garden and we enjoyed a pleasant half hour admiring the plants and asking questions. When the tour was over, we settled in the shade of the silver birch on the lawn, and she brought out a fresh jug of lemonade with ice cubes tinkling.

With Anxious getting fresh water from an outside

tap, we were all suitably refreshed and finally beginning to cool down.

"What brings you to these parts, may I ask?" inquired our generous host.

"It's another long story and another mystery," I admitted. "I seem to get embroiled in a lot of them."

"Max is like a real life Columbo," said Mum, beaming with pride. "Although much scruffier. He's been up to his neck in murders lately, but solved them all. He's great at it."

"Thanks, Mum."

"How exciting. Nothing much happens here, so please tell me. That sounded so gruesome at your campsite, but surely there isn't another murder?"

"We aren't exactly sure," I admitted. "You see, it all began with a note…"

As I told the story, it was clearly upsetting Constance as she turned almost white and drank endless glasses of lemonade. She rubbed at her throat and then her arms, red blotches like hives mottling her skin. I hurried through the rest, explaining about this being the only lead we got from Noel's wife.

"The man had a wife?"

"Yes, why?" I asked.

Constance shrugged. "I suppose I assumed he was single if he had the campervan and was travelling. Especially if he kidnapped someone."

"His wife said they usually travelled together, but once a year he pretended to have the campervan in for a service that took weeks. But it was an excuse to most likely get up to no good," said Dad.

"But we can't figure this out. It makes no sense how he could do it. Hiding someone in a campervan seems impossible. We came to the spot his wife told us was their favourite and where he would come alone for a few days sometimes, and although it's remote and private, it's still a massive risk, don't you think?"

"Way too big a risk. How very peculiar. But are you sure about this? Couldn't it just be a terrible mistake?" Constance rubbed her arms, the rash receding, but I still tried not to upset her so kept my tone light.

"It might be a strange joke. Someone might have been playing a trick on Noel, but that doesn't ring true. Now we found where he came, and I'm sure we got the right place, it's seeming much more likely that he did kidnap then murder someone. Have you heard about anyone disappearing recently? Maybe a few months to a few years ago?"

"Around here? No. Nothing like that. It's very quiet, with a few local villages, but I've not heard of anything so terrible."

"What about the clearing through the woods, and the path that leads here? Do you get many people passing by? Walkers, or possibly stealth campers?"

"I see the occasional walkers, but I can't say I ever saw a campervan. I go up there sometimes as it's such a lovely forest, but we are out of the way here."

"We?" asked Mum, eyebrows raised.

"Sorry, old habits die hard. I lost my husband three years ago and still talk like he's around. A slip of the tongue. It's why I moved here. A fresh start. Something to keep me occupied. It was the right decision, but I miss him dearly."

"We're so sorry for your loss." Mum smiled in sympathy and patted Constance's leg, the women clearly bonding.

"Thank you. But life goes on, and I keep busy, and have this wonderful garden. I count my blessings every day."

"That's the spirit," said Dad, finishing his lemonade then standing. "We've kept you long enough, but thank you for the drinks and the tour, and sorry for barging in like this. Bet we gave you a shock."

"No, not at all. It was nice to have the company."

"And sorry for the talk of death. We hadn't realised you'd lost your husband, and we kept talking about murder and kidnapping."

"Max, don't berate yourself. You weren't to know, and I'm afraid I'm rather squeamish. I hate to think of anything like that happening. It's truly terrible. But from the sounds of it, someone played a very bad joke on the previous owner of your campervan, and he never even knew."

"You might be right. Well, it was lovely meeting you."

"And all of you. Especially Anxious." Constance bent and stroked his head, then waved as we left her to continue murdering the weeds.

"She was a kind lady," said Dad as we retraced our route through the woods.

"And her garden was incredible." Mum grabbed Dad by the arm and pulled him to a stop. "Why don't we have a garden like that?"

"We have a lovely one, but who has the time?"

"You do. You don't have a job."

"Neither do you," countered Dad, the usual good-natured argument rearing its head once more.

"That's because I'm a savvy investor and taught Max everything he knows."

"I taught him all he needed to know about investing in property. That's why neither of us have regular jobs."

"You both taught me, and I appreciate it. Buying property and living off the rent is the best thing I could have done, and that's down to both of you. But we're getting sidetracked here. What did you really think about Constance?"

"How'd you mean, love?" asked Mum. "We just said. She was nice. Obsessive about the garden, but you'd have to be for it to look like that."

"Everyone needs a hobby," agreed Dad.

"I meant, you didn't find anything strange about her? Do you think she was telling us the truth?"

"Here we go." Dad rolled his eyes and walked off.

"Wait! What are you talking about?"

Dad spun and wagged a finger at me. "If you start speculating about maybe she was the kidnapper or has a house full of corpses, I don't want to hear it."

"Why would I do that?" I asked, genuinely interested.

"Dunno. But you were about to say something like that, weren't you?"

"I was just asking what you felt about her. If something seemed off."

"It didn't, so can we go now?" Dad stormed off in a huff, leaving me and Mum confused.

"Jack Effort, you come back here right this minute. You owe Max an apology and both of us an explanation. What's got into you?"

Dad trudged back, stamped his foot, and mumbled, "She was lovely. I don't want to think badly of everyone. I'm spooked, okay? This place is incredible, and I thought Max was going to spoil it by revealing something horrid about Constance."

"I wasn't. I'm not saying this is over, but maybe she was right and I'm overreacting to a dumb prank."

"I think you're probably right, love," said Mum. "You said it yourself that the police checked everything out and there was no sign of anything untoward. Sure, the husband lied about the yearly service, but maybe he wanted a break from home life and that was a white lie he told to get some space. Most likely, he fancied doing his own thing now and then without upsetting his wife."

"Let's just go home," I sighed. "Sorry for dragging you all over the place."

"We've had a lovely time, even if your dad is being

grumpy."

"I am not! I just want to think good thoughts about people. There's nothing wrong with that."

"Dad, you're right. Let's leave this behind us and get back home."

"But we want to stay until we solve the murder," insisted Mum.

"Course we do."

"I meant, home as in to the campsite. I think of each place I'm staying as home now."

Mum and Dad went off ahead with Anxious, leaving me to follow. I smiled privately to myself, having finally begun to figure out this perplexing mystery but not wanting to say a word until I was sure. But deep down, I already knew I was, and would return another day to clear up this terrible crime. For now, I wanted to enjoy my time with my parents and not think dark thoughts.

Emerging from the trees was like stepping into another world. Where there had been shadow, now there was intense, glorious light. The coolness vanished in a heartbeat, replaced with blistering temperatures. I wouldn't have been surprised to find the camper had melted, and I didn't fancy getting inside any time soon. We opened every door and window to get some air inside, and hung out for a few minutes in the shade as it was simply too intense to be out in the open.

We finally braved it, so we got in, closed everything, and I ramped up the vents to max. But this was not a modern vehicle and the "air con" was little more than like having tiny windows open, so instead we opened the main ones and tried not to think about the temperature, which didn't work in the slightest.

By the time I pulled up beside the pink death wagon, we were ready to combust. We couldn't get out fast enough, and retreated into the shade of the sun shelter and grabbed for cold water. Anxious had a drink then collapsed onto the rug and with a huff closed his eyes, as if daring anyone to speak to him or even consider disturbing him unless there were biscuits.

With a welcome glass of Prosecco, we slipped off our footwear and wiggled our toes in the grass—is there anything better in the whole world?

We sat in silence, slightly dazed from the strange afternoon and the punishing heat, so I sipped on the bubbly booze and watched life unfold around me.

But then I jumped up, almost spilling my drink before placing it on the table, and turned to my shocked parents. "What are we doing?"

"Don't know what you mean, love." Mum took a big gulp of her wine and smiled, a faraway look in her eyes.

"We're just settling down after a long day. It's nice to relax in the evening before we go for dinner at the restaurant. I might even have a wash first," laughed Dad, taking a big gulp like Mum.

"I think we've gone funny in the head," I grumbled, rubbing at my long hair then scratching my beard like it might awaken some sense.

"What's he on about?" Dad asked Mum.

"No idea."

"It's not the evening. We left mid-morning to go to the place Noel used to go, chatted with Constance for a while, then drove back. It's what, two o'clock?" I checked my watch again, and it really was.

"Don't be a pilchard, Max," warned Dad. "It's late. We ate while we were out. Or did we have a picnic? I can't remember?" He frowned, then turned to Mum to help him out.

"Um, not sure. Did you make lunch, Max? What did we have, love?"

"Nothing. We haven't eaten since breakfast. We're settling down with wine like it's been a full day, but it hasn't. It's only early. What is going on?" Deciding there was no point standing when I felt so beat, I resumed my sitting and had a drink.

"It's that weird place," said Mum. "We all felt it. It was magical, but I don't think it was the clearing so much as it was Constance's garden. It was the smell of the lovely flowers."

"Like a land that time forgot," sighed Dad.

"Don't you get any ideas about running off with another woman because she has a fantastic garden," warned Mum with a wag of her finger.

"Who said I was going to? I just liked her magnificent magnolias."

"Don't you dare talk about another woman's magnolias!"

"Her bushes were nice too," said Dad with a rapid wink at me before turning to Mum, face serious.

"You keep your eyes off her shrubbery," screeched Mum, cheeks burning as she wiped her lips then puckered up, smiling at Dad.

"I promise never to touch another woman's shrubbery," chuckled Dad.

With hunger pangs becoming insistent, I cobbled together a Ploughman's lunch that we tucked into eagerly, surprised how hungry we were.

Anxious remained on his side, unmoving, only his eyes wandering to follow the cheese, so he had a few sneaky nibbles, but bless him, his heart wasn't in it.

Energised by the food, drowsy from the wine, I cleared everything away while my parents relaxed, slowly coming back to myself from what felt like an utterly surreal morning. Almost as though it hadn't happened at all.

With the chores done, and life feeling normal again, I finished off my glass of wine, and with the reassuring snorts and grunts of my parents beside me, and Anxious whimpering as he chased rabbits in his dreams, I soon joined them and sank gratefully into a deep sleep.

Sometimes when you wake up after a nap you feel

refreshed, full of energy, and raring to go. This was not one of those times. I took an age to come around, and when I did, I was sweaty, groggy, rather dazed, and had a splitting headache.

Everyone else was fast asleep, so I left them in their rising pools of sweat and gathered my things quietly then went for a shower. It's always hit and miss at campsites regards water pressure, temperature, and cleanliness, but the shower block at The Poacher's Pitch was about as good as it got. Plenty of private stalls in a separate building to the toilets, which is always a bonus, and spotlessly clean.

The water was too hot if anything, so I turned it to cold and gritted my teeth, letting the strong spray sluice away the grime and rejuvenate me. After a thorough scrubbing, shampoo and conditioner for my hair and beard, then a brisk rub down with my towel, I applied beard oil, sorted out the knots, and finally dared to check myself over in the mirror.

Not too bad. My hair was past my shoulders when wet now, and looked darker until it dried, allowing me to pretend there were no streaks of grey at the sides. My beard was a touch too long, but still presentable enough, and my blue eyes had a strange, almost green appearance because of my tan. I might not be a male model, but I supposed I was okay for a man approaching mid-thirties and now living what was, admittedly, a much harder way of life than anything I'd ever done before.

Heading back to the pitch, I spied the detectives chatting with several guests I assumed they hadn't had the chance to speak to before, so dawdled then caught them up as they headed across the field towards my spot.

"Hi," I said brightly, genuinely pleased to see them.

"Hi!" they chorused, smiling. Still wearing workout clothes, they were as incongruous as ever, but their pleasant, relaxed manner was a welcome relief, especially because I hoped they had news that might help with the investigation.

"How's it going? Do you mind if I ask if you've discovered anything yet?"

"It's still early days, Max," said Sherry, glancing at Liam.

"Not much to report yet," he agreed, shaking his head almost imperceptibly at Sherry. "A day isn't long for these things. But time is of the essence."

"Agreed," chuckled Sherry. "The longer this goes on, the less chance of uncovering the truth."

"I told you about the hotdog factory, didn't I?" I asked, still rather befuddled.

"Yes, Max, you've been very forthcoming. And we told you we'd already been there and we'd been to Sunny Parks where the caravan came from. It all pans out. The son is rather flaky," whispered Sherry, leaning in after checking we weren't being overheard, "but I think that's just the kind of man he is. Nothing suspicious. We spoke to everyone, even the night shift at the factory, and nobody is missing. There's nothing strange we can see, and to be blunt, we're stumped."

"It's why we're here. To speak to the last few guests. Now we're done, and we agree that the chance of it being anyone who is staying here, or who left yesterday, is slim to none. The only ones who left were a family, and they had no chance to disappear and stew our victim. We also spoke to a man who was here for a day and he's a dead end too. He had issues at home and spent his time here drunk and brooding."

"So you don't think it was done at the factory? They have the equipment."

"They do, but it's the logistics, and it's too much of a stretch to be believable."

"The whole thing is unbelievable," I muttered.

"You got that right!" laughed Liam, his muscles flexing as he shook.

"What have you come up with then?" I asked. "I can't figure out how you would get the person inside on your own. Two killers?"

"Maybe, but again, that's a stretch. More likely, it was one strong person, or they planned this in advance and had something rigged up to get the body inside. But that's unlikely, as they didn't know the caravan was coming, did they?"

"No. Surely that means it must have been in there at Sunny Parks before my parents picked up the caravan?"

"Again, it's the logistics. There are a lot of people there, and Mike cleaned out the caravan the day before he handed over the keys, so unless the campsite owner's son lied about cleaning it, which we don't think he did, then we can't see how the body was put inside there."

"Thank you for sharing what you do know. I wish I had something to tell you, but I don't. I guess we'll just see what happens?"

"Sure, Max," said Sherry. "Don't beat yourself up over this. You can't win 'em all!"

"No, it's looking that way. Isn't this bugging you? How do you stew a body? Why? And who was killed?"

"Max, you would not believe how much this is annoying us," laughed Liam. "We have a perfect record when it comes to solving murders. Mostly because such crimes are so rare around here that there have only been a few cases over the years, but yes, it's annoying as hell. Something will turn up. It always does."

With nods of sympathy, as though I had lost a loved one, they both left.

I returned to the pitch more determined than ever to solve this.

Chapter 12

Everyone woke up when I returned, although Anxious did little but wag then collapse sideways again, clearly still in need of more rest. Mum and Dad fussed around getting their things together, then went for a shower, too, while I hung my wet towel out to dry and cleared up yet again.

Somehow, even though Mum's things were now in the caravan, she'd managed to make a mess in Vee again! Once sorted, I sat on the bench seat, rested my arm on the compact kitchen counter, and settled into silence.

Had my home really been the location of such horrible things? I tried to get a feel for any negative energy, but it was the same as it had always been. It felt like a happy place, warm and inviting, so old-fashioned it was retro cool. Dated, yet with modern touches to make it a true home, with no bad vibes whatsoever. How did I reconcile that with what had seemingly happened here?

Was Vee trying to right the wrongs inflicted on her by using me to solve murder mysteries, or was that fanciful thinking and a way to explain the madness that followed me around on my vanlife adventures?

I was beginning to think that it was nothing but a wild fancy, and this was, after all, merely a cool van. Of course it was! I'd let myself get carried away with reasons to explain how these things kept happening to me, when the truth was much simpler. Terrible things happen and I was either lucky, or unlucky, enough to be there to lend a hand figuring them out.

Going over the day's revelations once again, I knew I was right and that my suspicions were not only founded but true. I'd wait until my parents left, then put this confounding case to bed once and for all. But for now, we had more pressing problems, like figuring out who killed the mystery man.

Mum only took half an hour to get ready once they returned from their shower, a new record, but when she emerged from the caravan I couldn't help smiling.

"What are you grinning about?" she asked as she stepped down carefully, her red high heels giving her some much-needed height.

"You look amazing. I love the new bandanna. Yellow to go with your polka-dot dress. How can you get away with a white dress with yellow dots at a campsite? It's the opposite of what should work. You never seem to get muddy."

"I'm careful, and don't rub my hands over my clothes like you pair."

"Stop complimenting her," groaned Dad, nudging me in the ribs.

"Why? She looks nice."

"Because now if I compliment her, she'll say I'm copying you and didn't come up with the idea myself." Dad turned to Mum and said, "You look ace, love. Very pretty. Did you do something new to your hair?"

"You're only saying that because my sweet boy was so nice to his mum," snarled my crazy mother with a wink for me when Dad ducked to avoid the laser beams.

"See, I told you!" he grumbled, before rolling up the sleeves of his white T-shirt and patting his shiny hair.

"Are you wearing that, Max?" Mum gave me the once over, eyes disapproving, tone sharp enough to cut through three-day-old bread.

"Yes. Why?"

"It's very…"

"Suitable for a campsite and popping over to the pub for a bite to eat?"

"It's a restaurant, not a pub."

"It's a pub with a restaurant, so you can call it either. If you go for a drink, it's a pub. If you go for a drink and a meal, it's a restaurant," said Dad smugly.

"Restaurant," insisted Mum, daring anyone to counter her final offer.

"Restaurant it is," I laughed. "And I'm all dressed up. Black shirt, proper trainers."

"And cargo shorts."

"Yes, because it's still boiling hot. Shall we go? Where's Anxious?"

We searched for him, and after the third call he crawled out from under Vee, yawned, stretched, then trotted over, tail spinning, keen to see what the evening would bring.

We locked up, then took the short walk to the pub restaurant, and entered the small room where it was mostly locals sipping pints and chatting with the barmaid. Could it have been her? She was a slight woman, rather shy, with rosy cheeks, but seemed to know everyone and got on well with the customers. But Joni had said she was only nineteen and wasn't in the previous day, which was either suspicious or perfectly normal.

The only other people I hadn't spoken to were the barman and waitress, and apparently there was another man who helped out in the kitchen. If not this evening, then certainly tomorrow I would have to finish chatting to everyone I could think of, but for tonight I wanted to have a normal evening with my parents.

We took a table offered by the waitress and studied the menu. Anxious chose sausages, but he'd been eating too many so would have to make do with whatever leftovers there were this evening.

I chose a game pie, with roast potatoes and veg, not that I had high hopes if the previous meal was anything to go by. Mum and Dad both chose pork chops with mashed potatoes, gravy, and a selection of vegetables, even though I tried to dissuade them, suggesting that maybe something that didn't need perfect timing might be a better option. They would hear none of it, and I didn't push it, but my chef radar was on high alert when I saw what came out of the kitchen, and wished I'd insisted on cooking instead.

Joni appeared while we were waiting for our food, looking harried and unhappy. She almost passed us by, then noticed Mum and stopped to say hello.

"You look so pretty," said Joni, tugging at her own limp hair. "How do you do it?"

"This? Oh, it's nothing. Just threw it on." Mum waved dismissively, beaming at the compliment.

"I never get the time, and always smell of beer and the kitchen. It would be nice to dress up."

"You look lovely," said Mum. "So pretty, and you have the loveliest smile."

"Gosh, thank you. I haven't had a compliment for ages. Sorry, but we're rushed off our feet, and I need to help in the kitchen. Dan's in one of his moods again. And gosh, sorry again. I shouldn't be telling you these things. Enjoy your meal." Joni hurried off, tucking in her white blouse as she went.

"Trouble in paradise?" asked Dad with a frown as he picked up his fork then wiped it on a napkin that I trusted even less than the grubby cutlery.

"Looks that way. And why did she say they're rushed off their feet? There's us, a family, and two couples. That's not busy, is it, Max?" asked Mum.

"No, that's a quiet night. There are people drinking, too, but the barmaid deals with that. Maybe they're having issues."

"It'll be the upset from the murder," said Dad happily. "Always stresses you out."

"Since when have you had a murder on your business premises?" I teased.

"You know what I mean. I'm starving. I wonder how long it will be?"

"It should take at least twenty minutes, if not longer," I said.

"For a chop and a pie?"

"Yes. Dad, these things take time and you need to get it right. But my guess is it won't be very long." I excused myself and headed to the bathroom, but took the opportunity to take a wrong turn so I could get a peek into the kitchen. Joni and Dan were bickering as he absolutely ruined a rack of ribs, so she took over and deftly portioned them with a few expert cuts.

I slid away before I was seen, concerned about the state of the kitchen and Dan's inability to handle what should have been a simple piece of butchery. Sitting, I glanced at the passageway leading to the kitchen, not surprised to see the waitress carrying over the couple's meals even though they'd ordered moments before us.

No sooner had she returned to the kitchen than she was back again, this time with our food.

"Awesome!" exclaimed Dad. "I'm famished. Thanks, love. Looks like lovely grub."

"You're welcome, sir," said the waitress, her eyes red and her make-up smudged.

"You okay, my dear?" asked Mum, a little more observant than Dad who was already tucking in.

"Yes, fine. Thank you for asking. Do you need anything else?"

"No thanks." Once she'd left, Mum said, "She's been crying."

"Who?" asked Dad through a mouthful of food.

"The waitress, you blind fool."

"Had she?"

"Just eat your dinner. How is it?"

"Good mash and gravy. Haven't started the chop yet, but it looks tasty."

I inspected my own plate of food with a trained eye and was not impressed. To be sure, I cut into the pie, not surprised that no steam escaped. I was also gobsmacked to find barely any filling. Just a few tiny, generic pieces of meat that could have been absolutely anything. The roast potatoes were piping hot, though, but had that day-old taste so absolutely weren't cooked fresh, just re-heated.

"I wouldn't eat that if I were you," I sighed, putting my cutlery down.

"What you going on about?" spluttered Dad.

"It's not cooked. At least, mine isn't. And judging by the colour of that chop, your pork is half raw."

"Mine tastes lovely," said Mum, taking another mouthful.

I cringed as they ate, but tried again. "You know I was a professional chef at the very top of his game, right?" They mumbled they knew. "And I know this isn't fine-dining, but there are certain basics that everyone knows you adhere to. The most important is to ensure meat is cooked properly and hot all the way through. The chops aren't cooked. My pie isn't cooked. The potatoes aren't fresh, and who knows how old your mash is."

"Max, chill out," said Dad, looking cross. "Can't we just enjoy our meal? We know it isn't up to your standards, and you are an incredible cook, but this tastes nice. My meat is exactly how I like it. It's soft, well-seasoned, and good. Okay?"

"Okay. If you're sure."

My stomach flipped as I watched them eat, but I had to turn away. Maybe I was being judgemental, and if they said it was nice then that was what counted.

I noted the waitress removing plates from the

family's table, and the woman said something to her as she gathered up the still full crockery. She nodded, then hurried off. She returned a moment later, shaking her head, and the man snapped at her, voice low, but clearly angry. The waitress apologised, then came over to us as Mum and Dad had put their cutlery down and moved their plates away.

"Is everything okay here?" she asked.

Mum cast me a warning glance, and not wanting to upset the evening I told her we were fine and finished but asked if she was alright.

"Yes, I'm okay. We're having a busy night and some people seem to be in a terrible mood and not even very hungry. Weren't you?"

"Not very, no."

She cleared the table then left, but a commotion came from the kitchen and Dan, owner, chef, and grumpy guy stormed across the room and stood before me, arms folded, face sweaty, red, and angry.

"You didn't eat your pie."

"I know." I remained calm, but could tell this wouldn't end well.

"Why not?" he barked.

The restaurant went deadly silent; even the noise from the bar died down.

"I wasn't hungry."

"Liar! What, my food not good enough for an uppity, posh chef, eh? Think you're above me? Better than me and my lowly pub restaurant?"

"That's not it at all."

"You leave him alone," ordered Mum.

"There's no need for this, Dan," said Dad, using a tone that if he knew Dad would mean he'd know to cool it.

"I'll say whatever I want in my own place. Why didn't you eat your pie?" he demanded.

"It was cold, and there were only two tiny pieces of meat in it. The potatoes weren't even roasted today. I warned these two not to eat the chops, as they were utterly undercooked, but they did."

Dan's fists bunched and his face turned bright red as he trembled. "Why, you... How dare you!? I do proper food."

"Then tell me you cooked the potatoes today. Tell me you don't skimp on the meat in the pies. And tell me that you took proper care and attention with the chops."

"Those chops were perfect."

"Those chops were half frozen when you cooked them, so they weren't even properly hot in the middle. Same for the rest. You didn't cook anything fresh today, did you, apart from the vegetables?"

"The vegetables were frozen too," whispered Joni as she appeared beside her husband.

"You stay out of this. There's nothing wrong with using the freezer. So what if the chops were frozen? They were defrosted before I cooked them. And yes, the potatoes were from yesterday, but they were reheated in the oven. That's what lots of kitchens do."

"No, it isn't. They batch cook the same day then warm through, not food that's been left out for hours. You should be ashamed."

"That's it! I've had enough of you. I want you out of here right now and you can leave the campsite in the morning. You aren't welcome."

"Dan, stop it! Max and his parents are helping us. Stop overreacting. You know you aren't having a good day, so be honest."

"I'm fine. It's him."

"What about our food?" demanded the man with his family at the other table. "We complained, too, and said we wouldn't pay, but were told we had to. Our chops were half raw and cold, and the pie was pathetic. We feel cheated."

There were grumbles from another table, and all the while Joni was becoming more upset until she burst into tears, so did the waitress, and they hugged each other as Dan fumed.

Finally, he roared. "I'm done with this place. Do what you want," then tore off his apron, flung it at Joni, and stormed off. Everyone heard the door slam.

Noise levels rose as customers gossiped excitedly and Joni did the rounds, apologising to customers, and telling them they didn't have to pay. She was aghast at the poor food and swore it wasn't like Dan to be so lax, but I got the impression that she was lying and that he'd never served anything of decent quality. You would expect at least one or two regulars to be eating if that was the case, but as far as I could tell everyone was from the campsite or tourists. Locals stuck to drinking in the pub.

With the mood soured, we left. I had to carry poor Anxious as he was shaking. He hated arguments and knew everyone was angry, so needed plenty of cuddles and some extra attention before he calmed down then had a run around.

"That was a wild night," said Dad amiably as we opened up the vehicles.

"Wild? It was terrible," I sighed.

"Don't stress about it, Max. That guy's a joker and a right wally. Utter plonker if you ask me. He's too highly strung, and you're right, the pork chop was awful," he laughed.

"Then why did you eat it?" I asked, shocked.

"Didn't want to ruin it for this fine lady." He squeezed Mum's hand and smiled at her, the love evident.

"Mine was awful too," Mum admitted. "I only ate it as I didn't want to ruin it for Jack."

"What are you two like? But it's a shame we have to leave tomorrow. I feel bad for Joni."

"We're better off out of it," said Dad.

Joni arrived just then and got straight to the point. "I don't want you to leave. Dan was out of order and acted terribly. Please stay. I need you to figure out who killed that man."

"I don't see how we can, Joni. Dan owns this place, too, and was pretty clear what he thought about me."

"Let me speak to him. Please? I can't stand it that someone was killed. Please?"

"If you think it will help, but I don't fancy your chances."

"He's gone to his tent, like a child sulking. Let me convince him to apologise."

I nodded, so she walked with faltering steps over to the tent where Dan was sitting outside, staring at the ground, in-between swigging beer.

Mickey and Sue hurried over, and Mickey, blunt as always, said, "Blimey, guys, that was intense. We were at the door to the restaurant, and about to come in, when it kicked off. Was the food really that bad? We had lunch there the other day and it was okay, but a bit iffy. But that performance put us right off."

"It was awful," I admitted. "You were lucky you left it until late to eat."

"That man sounded so mean," said Sue. "He was so angry. Why did he behave like that?"

"Some people just aren't nice, love," said Mum. "Dan clearly has issues. I think the business is struggling, but that's still no way to act."

"It's sad that you have to leave," said Sue. "Have you found out anything about the murder yet?"

"Not yet." I glanced over with the others as Joni and Dan shouted at each other, then asked, "Have either of you heard anything?"

"Nothing, mate," said Mickey happily, tugging up his cut-offs, still not wearing a T-shirt.

"You aren't intrigued?" asked Dad.

"Sure I am. I've been asking around, but I didn't want to step on the expert's toes." He shrugged, smiling at me.

"Mickey is pretty good at it, but we haven't discovered anything."

"And I don't want to upset my gal by talking about murder constantly." He put his arm around Sue and she beamed at him. "See you later. And hopefully you won't have to leave tomorrow. Dan might cool down."

"Maybe, but if not, I'm sure we'll bump into each other again down the road."

"You can count on it."

I'd lost my appetite after the trouble, but fixed a sandwich and lamented not cooking a proper meal. One way or another, I was determined to make up for it tomorrow with something epic.

We settled down around a small campfire and talked while we sipped on wine and enjoyed what was left of the evening.

Then things became worrying. Anxious was the first to notice, but it didn't take long until the entire campsite was in turmoil.

Chapter 13

Dad shifted in his chair. Anxious whined then backed away.

"You okay?" I asked.

"Fine."

Anxious took another step, growling as his hackles sprang to attention. His head lowered while his backside rose. Either he was practising his yoga or something was up.

"What is it, boy?" I asked, checking we were alone.

Anxious yipped, eyes locked on Dad, then as Mum stirred from where she'd dozed off, he focused on her, eyes intent.

"That's a bit ripe," muttered Mum as she yawned then scrunched up her face.

Against my better judgement, I sniffed, and something truly noxious caught in the back of my throat like a rotten egg.

"Excuse me," mumbled Dad, wafting his hand then spluttering as his eyes began to water and he jumped from his seat. "Blimey, I'm really sorry. Bad case of wind."

"You stinky old man," hissed Mum, but then as she stood she let rip with a mighty trump and turned bright red. "Gosh, it must be contagious," she laughed.

"I think you two better take a few steps in that direction and get ready to run," I said, standing and shifting sideways so I didn't get the full brunt of their gaseous emanations and pointed towards the toilet block.

Shouts rang out around the campsite, then the couple who'd argued with Dan raced towards the toilets, trying to hold both their bums and mouths at the same time, making for some very interesting movements. I stifled a laugh as I was reminded of penguins shuffling through the snow, and wouldn't have been surprised to see them try to slide along on their bellies.

"I don't feel so well," said Dad, now a worrying shade of green.

Mum's pale skin was almost translucent except for two bright spots burning her cheeks, so red they were nearly luminescent. "Me either. My tummy feels funny and I think I might need the loo."

"You've both got food poisoning. You'd better grab some clean underwear, all the toilet paper, and I do mean all of it, and get going before the entire campsite is fighting over toilet access. Prepare to pray to the porcelain gods."

They exchanged a worried look, then jumped into action and gathered what they needed. With much trepidation, my folks waddled towards the toilets in a terrifying race against others emerging from tents or bent double and already halfway there. John, the lone hiker and keen map reader, was going so slow it was clear he wouldn't make it.

I heard the eruption from the other side of the field. John wailed as things were let loose from both ends in an admittedly impressive display as he clutched at his backside and vomited violently.

Food poisoning was no joke, and I felt no sense of smugness even though I'd warned my parents, as it was a truly horrible experience. You felt like you were going to die, that this was the end, and it truly couldn't get any worse. But it could, and it did, and it left you weak, beyond sick, and utterly drained.

It could also be life-threatening, but that was rare and everyone seemed to be in fine health before they contracted it. I collected together towels and flannels, sorted out separate water bottles for people to sip on, and fished out electrolyte sachets and dissolved them in the water. They would become very dehydrated and needed to drink as much as they could during this first rough bout.

I told Anxious I wouldn't be long, then headed over to the busy facilities and called in to tell Mum and Dad I was outside if they needed me, hoping they wouldn't, knowing that after what they'd done for me over the years when I got ill, I had to brave this and be there for them.

My fingers were crossed, though, as the noises and smells coming from inside were beyond unpleasant.

The campsite was in uproar, with concerned people either coming to investigate or to use the bathrooms, and I had to explain to a few that there was a case of food poisoning and to ensure they washed their hands thoroughly. Mickey and Sue turned up and I told them to be sure not to eat at the restaurant, and if they felt unwell to be prepared for the worst.

"That idiot Dan shouldn't be allowed to serve food. Look what he's done," said Mickey, serious for once.

"He should have known better," I agreed. "Accidents happen, but he was very lax and knew things weren't right."

"This is awful. How could he not cook the food properly?" asked Sue.

"My guess is that this isn't the first time." I glanced towards his tent, but he was nowhere to be seen.

Joni Chin arrived, more distraught than ever, and marched over to us. "What's happening? Is everyone sick?"

"Food poisoning," I explained, knowing no more needed to be said.

"That utter idiot. I can't believe he's done this again!" Joni's hand slapped to her mouth as her eyes widened, then she sighed, her shoulders sank, as she admitted, "Yes, it's happened once before. I warned him to take his time, that this was unacceptable, but he got angry and blamed the supplier. That stupid man. This is the end of us now. We'll be ruined. They'll shut us down and we won't have a business. First the murder, and now this. We're done."

"Hey, what's going on?" asked Mike, Joni's son, as he joined us, stifling a yawn. His hair was mussed and he wore a grey dressing gown so had clearly been in bed.

"Your Dad poisoned most of the campsite," said Mickey happily, his good humour returning.

"He did it again?" Mike asked Joni. "He wouldn't listen, would he? Wouldn't let me work here. I told him I wanted to take over in the kitchen, but neither of you think I'm smart enough."

"It isn't that at all," protested Joni. "We just know you're better with people than in the kitchen."

"Don't trust me, more like. Think I'm useless. Now look what he's done. You can say goodbye to the business now." With a scowl, Mike stormed off, the belt of his dressing gown trailing along behind him.

"Your boy really wants to work here, eh?" asked Mickey.

"He does, but it never worked out. He's not the best with numbers, and although he's a fine cook he can't stick to a system and gets confused about the timings. It was an utter disaster when he was running the kitchen, even with us helping. That's why Dan took over again, but he's made a terrible mess of things this time. Sorry, you don't want to hear any of this. I'm mortified about the trouble. This is the worst holiday ever for our guests, and it's our fault."

"Joni, you aren't the ones who murdered anyone," I said, leaving the inevitable question of, "Were you?" hanging without asking it.

"Were you?" asked Mickey, blunt as always.

"Mickey, you can't say that!" warned Sue, slapping his arm.

"What? I'm just asking."

"No, I didn't kill anyone. Neither did Dan nor my boy. This is too much for me. I need to find Dan and get him to sort this mess out."

"There's not much you can do now," I explained. "As long as everyone was in good health otherwise, they should be fine in a few hours. They'll be weak, and not feeling their best, but by tomorrow everyone should be on the road to recovery."

"Yeah, and on the road high-tailing it out of here."

"I can't blame them," sighed Joni. With a sad shake of her head, she rushed to Dan's tent, went inside, then emerged and looked around the campsite.

"Wonder where that idiot's got to?" asked Mickey. "Bet he heard people being ill and scarpered."

"Maybe. Or he's gone to drown his sorrows somewhere. This doesn't seem like a very happy place."

"Let's leave Max to help Jack and Jill, Mickey," said Sue. "It's time for us to go to bed."

"See you in the morning," I said, then took a deep breath and went to check on my shouting parents.

Over the next few hours, things went from bad to worse to not so bad at all actually, to utterly horrifying when I had to enter the stall my mother was in. Some things a son should never have to witness, but witness them I did, even surviving to tell the tale, although the scars shall always remain.

Dad was even worse, having absolutely no qualms about requesting assistance, unlike Mum who was utterly mortified until I insisted she let me help her.

Things gradually eased off and after a few false starts of returning to our pitch then having to hurry back to the now thankfully quieter toilet block, the worst seemed to be over. Gradually, the campsite finally settled down as people retreated to tents and more robust enclosures, praying they wouldn't have to make a dash for it in the middle of the night.

It was not to be, and every so often someone would

hurry from their tent, head torch lighting the way, muttering to themselves or crying out, disturbing everyone's restless night once again. The only saving grace was that at least not everyone staying had eaten at the restaurant, so the toilets were free when needed. I couldn't have imagined the carnage otherwise.

At about three in the morning, with Mum and Dad collapsed in chairs, half delirious with cramps and sweating badly but their temperatures not worryingly high, I noted Joni hurrying towards Dan's tent.

The lights from the toilet and shower blocks had remained on all night, and as he was at the far end the tent was lit up enough for me to see her pause outside, glance around, then duck inside.

Shrouded in darkness, I was unseen, and I wondered what she would say if he had finally returned to his tent. With so much coming and going through the night, I had no idea if he was inside or not, and had dozed off numerous times. Everyone else was asleep now, but rest eluded me as I worried about my parents and puzzled over the mysterious murder.

A piercing scream filled the night air, startling roosting birds that flapped from the trees. In moments, lights at campervans and tents were turned on and I hurried towards Joni as she staggered from the tent, stumbled, and fell face forward after tripping over Dan's camping chair.

Anxious howled and I called for him to follow as I pelted across the field and helped a trembling Joni to stand. Her head torch blinded me as I asked, "What happened? Are you hurt? Was there an argument?"

"No. He's... he's dead!" Joni turned to stare at the tent, but I kept hold of her as her knees give way. Taking her weight, I held her upright then she batted at me with small hands and wailed, "Why did he have to die?" before clutching me tight and sobbing into my chest.

"Wait here," I said, then gently moved her hands and turned on my own head torch before approaching the tent flap. With a nervous gulp, I tore it aside, the unmistakable smell of blood filling my nostrils.

Dan was rigid on top of his sleeping bag, clothes and paraphernalia strewn around him. His arms and legs were tight by his side, his legs closed. I noted several books, an empty bottle of vodka, a mixer, and glasses on a low camping table, along with a torch, a light to read by, and, strangely, his gold wedding ring. My eyes returned to Dan's corpse, his shirt soaked with blood, a large knife plunged to the hilt in his chest.

Stepping back cautiously, I emerged to find Joni swamped by people. Mickey and Sue were consoling her, Mum and Dad were confused and not looking well at all, and several other campers were just as befuddled after their illness.

Mike appeared in his dressing gown and shoved through the small group and shouted, "What's he done now?"

"Mate, your dad's dead," said Mickey, draping an arm over Mike's shoulder.

"He's not dead! He's probably drunk. Let me see." Mike brushed Mickey aside and flung the tent flap wide open for everyone to see. People gasped, Mike stepped inside the tent cautiously, stared down at his father's body, then backed out, turned to Joni, and asked, "Did you kill him?"

"What!? No, of course not. I came to try and find him as he'd been gone for hours, and he was like that. Dead. Same as the other man. Has he, you know, been cooked?"

"Just stabbed. Not stewed to the bone," confirmed Mickey with rather too light a tone.

"This is madness," sighed Mike, slapping at his cheeks as if he could wake from a dream. "Who would do this? Is it because of the food?" he wailed. "You! I bet it was you!" he snarled, pointing at first me, then a very bewildered John.

"I need to call the police. And I need a drink," said

Joni numbly.

"I'll take you, love," offered Mum.

"No, I'll be fine. Everyone please return to your pitch. The police will be here soon, but stay together and nobody touch anything."

Joni stumbled off, head torch lighting her way.

Mike remained motionless, staring at the tent like it had answers, but it didn't, and neither did anyone else.

"You okay, love?" Mickey asked Sue, who, like Mike, was fixated on the tent.

She turned, smiled weakly, and said, "What? Oh, yes. Better than him. Let's get into the Dub. I don't like it out here." Sue cast around, looking at everyone, then huddled close to Mickey as he escorted her back to their home and hopefully to safety.

"What's a Dub?" whispered Mum.

"Short for VDub, as in VW. There's a whole world of slang for people really into my make of campervan."

"Oh, right. Um, I need to go." Mum's skin drained of all colour as she waddled off.

"Wait for me," wailed Dad, his colour the opposite and rising as he sped after her.

And so the second wave began, and it was worse than the first.

Fifteen minutes later, I heard sirens approaching, and the field lit up like day. I turned, and walked back across the grass with Anxious right by my side, the poor guy utterly bewildered and confused by such activity at an hour when he would normally be oblivious to the world. At the entrance to the field, I understood why it was suddenly so bright.

Joni and Mike were running away from their home and business, dark silhouettes stark against a blazing inferno as the entire building was engulfed in flames. Already licking at the thatched roof, the windows were smashed and fire and smoke billowed out as the crackle and roar became deafening.

We hurried to intercept the understandably terrified mother and son, and met up on the track.

"Are you okay?"

"Yes, I think so," stammered Joni. "Mike, are you hurt?"

"No. Just utterly freaked out. First Dad, now this? Someone's really got it in for us. Maybe we're next?"

"Maybe they tried to kill us," shuddered Joni. "Max, did you see anything? I was having a drink to settle my nerves, Mike was in the back getting me a blanket, then the whole place erupted in flames. I'd moved into the restaurant, just looking around, I guess because I knew our life was truly over, but then there was an explosion and... and..."

"Mum, it's okay. Come on, let's go and sit down."

A window blew out and the fire raced up the side of the building, the roof already half gone as more explosions rocked the campsite.

Joni screamed, we all ducked, and the heat became intense so we moved to the campsite where everyone had gathered at the entrance, mesmerised by the fire and this latest development at what truly had to be the unluckiest campsite in the country.

"First poor Dan, and now this. There's nothing left. Nothing at all." Joni sank to her knees, sobbing.

Mike looked at me as if I could fix this, then sat beside his mother and held her as she cried, her wails drowned out by the approaching sirens of police cars and ambulances, and hopefully the fire brigade.

Vehicles poured into the campsite, racing past the inferno, and teams of officers hurried from their vehicles, immediately surrounded by the guests. I left Mike and Joni, and went to find Mum and Dad, relieved to see that they were alright and their spirits higher. But it was short-lived as we met in the middle of the field and they realised that things had taken yet another terrible turn.

I explained about the fire, and they wanted to see, so we dodged vehicles and waited with everyone else, watching the building turn from a quaint stone edifice hundreds of years old, into little more than a blackened shell within minutes. The fire had spread incredibly fast, most likely because of the alcohol, and there would be drums of oil for the kitchen, some clearly having been stored outside and caused the fire to rage on all sides.

I worried about gas lines, or oil tanks for heating, too, but there were no further explosions.

As officers tried to make sense of the situation, the fire department arrived and scores of brave souls set about trying to get the fire under control as hoses were reeled out and huge arcs of water doused the building, slowly turning it into a smouldering ruin of a life now gone forever.

"Come on, let's get you two back to our pitch. How are you feeling?"

"Better than Dan, worse than you," grumbled Dad.

"I feel good, actually," chirped Mum, smiling at me.

"Then let's hope that's the food poisoning over with."

Anxious led the way, keen to put as much distance between himself and the chaos as possible.

I sat with him in my lap and slowly he calmed then curled up and was soon fast asleep. It had been a busy night for everyone, and would continue to be so for many hours to come.

Chapter 14

Vehicle headlights lit up the campsite, yet Anxious continued to sleep through the ensuing chaos as more people arrived, including the detectives. Dan's tent was cordoned off and teams went about the laborious process of checking over the scene, while officers spoke to everyone, slowly unravelling the whole sorry story that began with food poisoning and ended with murder and fire.

Every so often, someone would rush to the toilets, but as dawn broke, the worst of it was over and my folks had recovered remarkably well, although left with cramps, the occasional gurgle, and some serious sweating.

I spoke to a few uniformed officers, told them my side of the story, but didn't get the opportunity to speak with the detectives for several hours. It was only once I set up for coffees for as many people as I had cups that they finally came over to chat.

After the long line of officers and campers had been given a drink, they gladly took one themselves and we moved aside to talk in private.

"Well?" asked Sherry Hay, hands on hips.

"This better be good," sighed Liam Ram with a weak smirk. His eyes remained full of mirth, as though he was deciding whether to share an inside joke that was never forthcoming.

"Why are you talking like I have all the answers? I was dealing with my parents, then Joni found Dan. She was distraught, so went inside to fix a drink. Mike joined her, then they came running out because the house was on fire."

"Yes, we know that," said Sherry. "What we don't know is who killed Dan, or who burned the house down."

"So it was arson?" I'd guessed it was, and had a suspicion of who it might have been, and why, but it was good to have it confirmed.

"Max, don't play dumb," said Liam. "If you're as great as any detective, then you know for sure it was arson. We don't like coincidences, and this would be a massive one if it was an accident. So stop messing about and speak your mind."

"I didn't want to jump to any conclusions."

"That's admirable, but you know to go with your gut, same as we do. Don't take us for fools after we've been so helpful."

"I wasn't. I'm trying to get things straight in my head, but it's a lot to take in. Dan and Joni had a massive argument after the incident at the restaurant, which I'm sure you heard about."

"We did." Sherry nodded.

"Then he went to his tent to sulk and drink. But he disappeared at some point. She was looking for him, but nobody had seen the guy. Everyone was coming and going, feeling sick, then she came over about three this morning and found him inside. Mike turned up not long after. He assumed his dad was drunk again, and he wasn't too happy about it."

"So, what's the deal?" asked Liam.

"Right now, I'm not certain of anything. But I have my suspicions."

"I knew it!" laughed Liam, and lifted a muscular arm to high-five Sherry, then turned to me. "Don't leave me hanging, Max. That ain't cool."

I reluctantly slapped palms, then asked, "Do you have any suspects?"

"We're detectives. We suspect everyone. Even you, Max," giggled Sherry.

"I can't figure you two out. Why are you always so cheerful and happy to talk about the case? How are you so fit? Detectives are never like you."

"We broke the mould," said Sherry, then they high-fived again. "But seriously, this is becoming very annoying. Too many bodies, Max, and we don't like fire. It complicates things."

"It sure does," agreed Liam.

"How so?"

"More work for us. Now we have to figure out who committed three crimes rather than two. Our boss is already close to a coronary as *his* boss is breathing down his neck. Now we'll be under more pressure. Which means we want this sorted. We even missed a few workouts because of this, and these guns don't grow on trees."

"No, but your legs look like trees," said Sherry, eyeing up Liam's muscular thighs clad in shiny black training shorts.

"Kind of you to say so," he beamed, flexing his quadriceps like that was a natural thing and anyone could do it.

"We have quite a few suspects," I admitted. "For a while, I considered Dan because he clearly wasn't happy with how things were here. But the main suspect had to be his son, Mike. He had access to the caravan. There were family issues, and he obviously resented his parents. A happy home this is not."

"And he isn't the smartest," said Liam.

"No, but I think he's a decent enough guy. Even Joni could have done it to give the place notoriety. Some people actively seek out murder scenes and maybe she thought it would give the failing business a boost."

"Not very likely, but yes, it's a possibility," conceded Sherry.

"And now her husband is dead. They argued, and he ruined the business with the food poisoning."

"But she wasn't around when he was murdered, was she?"

"Who knows? People were coming and going and it was hard to keep track. But Joni was insistent I stay and help figure out who the murderer was, even when Dan told us to leave. She wanted the killer caught. It could have been anyone."

"But it couldn't have been, could it?" said Sherry with a smirk. "The staff weren't around all night. They were at home. We checked, and they have alibis. Everyone was with a spouse, partner, or parent. There aren't that many people who work here, and they're accounted for. So it means it was someone at the campsite."

"Maybe, but it could also have been someone from Sunny Parks come to try to distance the business after whatever went wrong that led to the body being in the caravan. And let's not forget the hotdog factory."

We glanced over at the pink beast. Mum and Dad waved back happily, clearly over the worst now and sipping on milky, and no doubt very sweet, tea.

"There are some right characters at Sunny Parks," said Liam, "but, again, it doesn't feel right. Gut instinct."

"And you're certain about the staff from here?" I asked. "I was going to speak to them today, but they have alibis?"

"Unless everyone we spoke to was lying, then yes, they're in the clear. Which brings us right back to the people here or someone we've overlooked entirely," said Sherry.

"The sausage factory is still a worry," said Liam.

"It's not sausages, it's hotdogs."

"They do sausages too."

"Yes, but it's mostly hotdogs, or Frankfurters,

whatever you want to call them. Ugh, horrid things."

"Not everything has to be health food," said Liam with a *tsk*.

"Okay, I'll leave you to your discussion about healthy food and get back to my folks now, if that's okay?"

"Sure, Max, but don't go solving this without us. Don't want to look bad in front of the others." Liam shook my hand, then glared down and pulled out a small bottle of antiseptic gel and cleaned both of his thoroughly. "Just in case. You might be contagious."

"I didn't eat my food."

"No, but you touched lots of things, I bet. Stay safe, and be well. And call me." Liam held a pretend phone to his ear and winked.

I left them discussing the fat and salt content of hotdogs and staggered over to the beautiful aroma of coffee.

"Figured you'd need it, Son," said Dad with a sympathetic smile as I sank gratefully into a chair.

"Thanks. Wow, is it really eight already?"

"Already?" grumbled Mum. "That was the longest night of my life except when I had you. I could sleep for a week."

"Let's agree that we're tired, but at least Max wasn't poorly."

"How are you both doing now?"

"We're on the mend. That was a terrible business, but I'm sure we'll be as right as rain soon enough," said Dad happily.

"You don't feel wretched?"

"Absolutely abysmal. Truly awful," he laughed. "But we're alive, and that's the most important thing. That Dan wasn't a nice bloke, but he didn't deserve to be murdered. This place is starting to freak me out."

"Maybe it's best you go home. You need to rest after the food poisoning, and I'm worried something might happen."

"You can't get rid of us that easily," snapped Mum.

"I'm just thinking about you." I was shocked by her reaction, as she seemed genuinely angry.

"Then don't. We're older than you, and have been around. We can look after ourselves."

"What's wrong?"

"Nothing."

"Mum, tell me."

"We're worried about you, okay? You say you're concerned about us? Imagine how we feel. We're your parents, so we worry."

"Always have, always will," agreed Dad.

"I'm fine. You know I can handle myself."

"Until you can't. Then what?"

"Then nothing. Anxious will protect me, won't you?" I looked down, but he was fast asleep.

Mum grunted, as if that proved her point.

They were clearly out of sorts, but I didn't push it. If they wanted to stay, I was happy for them to be here, but it was definitely a concern, and a pressing one. The longer the killer remained at large, the more risk there was of something happening to one, or both, of them. This needed to be dealt with, and fast.

While they showered and changed, and tried to put the night behind them, I did the rounds of the campsite, checking on everyone, trying to get information but being discreet. Nobody saw anything I hadn't seen myself, and nobody had noticed Dan returning to his tent in the night.

"What are you looking so worried about?" asked Mickey.

I glanced up to find him and Sue standing before me, arm in arm, smiling.

"None of this is your fault, you know?" Sue smiled wanly, then her eyes lit up and she asked, "Is there anything we can do to help?"

"Yes, mate," blurted Mickey. "Let us give you a

hand. I'm itching to help solve the killings and catch whoever set fire to the pub."

"As long as it isn't too gruesome," said Sue.

"Are you sure?" I asked her. "I thought the talk of murders upset you too much?"

"It's not the talk of murders. It's when too much detail is discussed. But Mickey's keen to help out, and I'm trying to be more supportive. Maybe we can help you look for clues? That's what you were thinking, isn't it? I recognise that look, Max. I've seen it on you before. You're getting close, so let us help."

"I could do with a few more pairs of eyes." I explained my thoughts about how the bodies were placed, and Mickey was almost beside himself with joy when I asked if they'd hunt around the woods with me to see what we might find.

"Sounds awesome, mate. Let's do it!"

"Me too," said Sue, pulling Mickey tighter, smiling nervously as she glanced into the trees.

"You do both realise that this might be dangerous? Whoever is doing this might strike again. I get the feeling they won't, at least not now, but I don't want to go another day, and certainly not a night, without this maniac being found. You're okay with that?"

"We are," said Sue, eyes meeting mine. I read the determination, the lack of fear, and it was like she was a different person. Maybe she'd had time to get used to Mickey talking about murder, or maybe she'd simply had enough, or maybe it was something else, but she wanted this. Possibly even needed it.

We hung around until the crazy parents arrived, and they were more than happy to stay put, Mum waving us off with a cheery, "You kids have fun."

"She's a right character. Your dad too," said Mickey once we were out of earshot and into the trees.

"You wouldn't believe half the stories if I told you," I said, trying to take in everything I saw.

"Try me," he teased. "My folks are just proper boring. They never do anything, and hate that Sue and I live like this. They think we're utter dropouts. Never mind that we have jobs and work from our laptops. They think it's a disgrace."

"They might come around."

"They haven't yet, but that's their problem, not mine. Come on, tell us a tale about your crazy folks, Max."

I thought for a moment, then smiled as I recalled a perfect example of what it had been like growing up and living with less than conventional parents.

"I must have been thirteen or fourteen and it was parents' evening. All the teachers were in the assembly room sitting at desks and people had an appointment booked to talk to them."

"I remember those. It was always excruciating, especially if you were made to go," said Mickey.

"Yes, well, this one was in the evening so I had to go too. My folks were going out dancing afterwards, and I was going to be given a treat if my reports were good. But they didn't want to have to go back home to get changed, so they dragged me along and I was utterly mortified. They rocked up in their finery and barged into the assembly room laughing and joking, really excited to speak to the teachers and then go out. I was going to be dropped off at my uncle's afterwards, which I was looking forward to as he's a great guy."

"That doesn't sound so bad," said Sue.

"No? I was absolutely mortified. The entire room fell silent. All the teachers, parents, and children turned to look at us. My folks were utterly oblivious, and were joking about. Mum was telling Dad that he needed to practice more, so that's what they did. Right there and then. A massive room, everyone looking, the others in regular clothes, and Mum in a bright red evening gown, Dad with his usual fifties look but wearing a dinner jacket, hair slicked back, and they began jiving. He was twirling her around, she was singing at the top of her lungs, and they just didn't care."

"That's so awesome!" laughed Mickey.

"It is not!" I chuckled, shaking my head at the memory. "It was then that I realised they'd always be different, and up until then I was embarrassed by how they dressed and how different they were to my friends' parents. But this was so overboard that I accepted who they were and there was no reason to care what anyone else thought. Mind you, it took a while for that to sink in. When it happened, I wanted to go and hide in a corner."

With our spirits lifted, and Sue much more relaxed, we began to search the woods. There was little to do but walk around, following animal tracks or ducking beneath branches and checking the ground. I wasn't even sure what we were looking for, just that with nothing else to do and nowhere else to go, this was as good an idea as any.

Police had already searched the entire area, teams skirting the bordering fields and the woods, but they'd come up with nothing. Why did I think we'd fare any better? Instinct. That's all it was. The belief that there must be something somewhere. After having circled the entire campsite, we regrouped, then decided to investigate deeper into the trees.

Anxious led the way, seeming to have more of an idea where we were going than us, and soon we found ourselves deep into the strange twilight world of the forest. The sounds of the campsite receded, the acrid tang of smoke fading until it became like a dream and it was hard to reconcile the peace with the chaos that had preceded it.

Swallowed up by the trees, with soft moss underfoot that had continued to thrive thanks to the cooler air beneath the dense canopy, we made no sound as we trailed Anxious, his nose to the ground, following an almost invisible path that weaved around ancient trees and led us further away from the scene.

We must have walked for at least a mile, yet I felt

determined to carry on. If nothing else, Anxious was having a wonderful walk, and I was reluctant to return to the campsite with all the people and upset. If I was being honest with myself, more than anything I wanted to get the smells gone. After a night of dealing with severe food poisoning and being in close, way too close, proximity to everyone, it had left a very nasty tang that was only just clearing.

"Max, mate?" Mickey and Sue had paused, both frowning.

"Yes?" I asked, stopping and turning.

"Think that's enough? There's nothing out here."

"And we're a long way from the campsite now," said Sue. "We aren't exactly dressed for a hike. We've all got Crocs and shorts on and Mickey doesn't even have a T-shirt."

"I'm a free spirit. Clothes are too restricting."

"Yes, Mickey, I know you think that. But when you're in the woods sometimes more clothes are just sensible. I think we should go back."

"Sorry, yes, you're right. We should go." But something tugged at me, and I remained rooted to the spot. What was it?

Anxious barked from the other side of an ancient dry stone wall.

Chapter 15

Mickey grinned, Sue flushed as her eyes darted back and forth, and I got a tingle. A full body one. I had to investigate.

"A clue?" asked Mickey, rubbing his hands together.

"I think so, yes."

"We should leave. We've been gone ages and the ground is getting rough. Let's go back," stammered Sue.

"Babe, it's fine." Mickey draped an arm over her shoulders and promised, "Nothing will happen. Max and I won't put us in danger."

"But what if the killer's there?" she asked, glancing at the wall.

"Come on, it'll be fun. You said you wanted more adventure. Now here it is."

Sue reluctantly let Mickey take her hand and they followed as I turned back to the wall and approached cautiously.

Anxious' barking became more insistent before he leaped the wall and landed in front of us, panting happily, tail wagging, utterly oblivious to the scare he'd caused.

"Blimey!" laughed Mickey nervously. "I nearly had a heart attack. You okay, babe?"

"Fine. Let's get this over with."

With a nod, I hurried after Anxious who'd vanished again. The first thing I saw was not a derelict farmhouse or ancient cottage as I'd imagined, but a massive pit. An old mine shaft or small-scale quarry, possibly, but it was so overgrown with weeds and covered in moss and lichen that it clearly hadn't been disturbed for decades.

"Careful," I warned, remaining on the safe side of the wall.

"It's just a hole," said Mickey glumly.

"But there's a shack over there. I think Anxious wants us to investigate."

Mindful of our step, and keeping well away from the piles of rocks and the roughest ground, we instead followed a path that had clearly been used recently.

"What's going on here?" asked Mickey.

"No idea. But it can't be a coincidence."

"I don't like this," whispered Sue. "It's dangerous. Let's go."

"I don't mind if you want to," I said. "I'll see you both soon."

"No way! This is the real deal, Sue. But if you're worried, take a seat and we'll only be a minute. We need to check this place out. We might discover something. This is how Max operates, right, Max?"

"It does seem to be important." I shrugged, aware that Sue was uncomfortable and not wanting to do anything to scare her.

"Fine. Sorry. I got spooked, but you're right. This could be a clue."

Anxious was sniffing at the rotten base of the door to a weathered but still relatively sound looking shack. Little but an oversized shed, it was a peculiar mix of tin and wood, with repairs carried out over the years with little concern for aesthetics. I couldn't imagine what on earth it had been used for, but rather than try the door, we chased after Anxious when his head suddenly snapped up and he tore around the side of the building.

"He's on to something!" gasped Mickey, then gave chase, leaving Sue behind.

"Sorry, but we need to take a look. Would you rather wait by the wall?" I asked.

"No, I'm coming."

Before I could try to stop her, Sue hurried past me. I followed behind, eyes trying to take in everything at once in case we weren't alone.

I stopped just before I bumped into the pair under a tin roof at the rear of the building.

Something large and bloody was hanging from a long pole supported between the rafters, with smaller prey in various stages of drying. Pots, pans, knives, hooks, and a chunky bench were dotted around a small camp of sorts, with a huge metal container easily big enough to fit half a dozen people inside standing proudly in a cleared area.

Surrounded on all sides by trees, you would never know this place was here unless you were told, and yet there was a clear path through the undergrowth leading into the woods further along.

"This is freaky, man," whistled Mickey, cuddling Sue in close.

"Anxious, stay with us, please," I asked as I nodded to them then joined him over by the large carcass.

It was a deer, already dressed after the hunt. The long bench was stained dark from years of butchering, with viciously sharp knives lined up along with a cleaver and even saws.

"What is this place?" asked Sue.

"My guess is it's an illegal hunter's hideout. Someone likes to hunt and prepares the meat here."

"What about that?" asked Sue, pointing at the huge metal drum with a series of peculiar chimneys spaced evenly around it. A ladder lay beside it, presumably to access the inside.

"That's for making charcoal," said Mickey with pride as he puffed out his chest, pleased to contribute.

"How do you know that?" I asked.

Mickey shrugged. "Saw this show on TV about a guy who lived in the woods in Wales. He made his own charcoal. It's pretty cool. You make this massive fire in the huge drum, get it up to temperature, then put the lid sections on. He had to stay with it all night and adjust the airflow using dampers in the chimneys or moving the lids. Otherwise, it could turn to ash. If you do it right, you get incredible charcoal. Or maybe it's called biochar. I guess someone does that here. Ah, it's called a ring kiln."

"Or uses it to steam people," I said. "We need to be careful. Don't touch anything, but we should look inside the shack."

Anxious was whining by the meat, but it wasn't good now. It must have been here for a few days and someone had planned on returning, so I tempted him away with a biscuit which he devoured hungrily, then let him lead the way to the front of the building.

Cautiously, I eased the door open to reveal a cosy interior with several chairs, a makeshift table made from scrap wood, and even cutlery and crockery stacked on a plank used as a counter.

It was very rundown and clearly didn't get used like the outside did, and there was nowhere to sleep, which surprised me. Nobody was here, and there was nothing to suggest who used the shack or hunted illegally, so we left and I closed the door.

"Blimey, this is giving me the heebie jeebies," shuddered Mickey.

"It's a peculiar setup. This is either important or nothing to do with what's been happening. But someone is hunting illegally and wants to stay hidden."

"Who would do this?" asked Sue.

"Maybe someone lives in the woods," suggested Mickey. "A gnarly grizzled dude with hair down to his ankles, living off the land."

"But there's nowhere for him to stay," said Sue.

"Maybe he lives well away from here to avoid getting caught. He might just come to process the meat and make his charcoal."

"Or she. It might be a she," corrected Sue.

"Could be, babe. Yeah, you're right. Let's get out of here, though. This place is utterly gross and freaky."

"Give me one minute. I need to check something out first," I said, then hurried around to the back.

The charcoal drum was an immense thing. The large lid sections were scattered seemingly randomly to the side. Only because of my height was I able to peer inside. It was empty bar a coating of charcoal at the base, but there was still residual heat when I bent to check the bottom of the drum. With a raging fire inside, then left to work its magic for a day or more, I assumed it would take several days for the temperature to return to normal. But when was the charcoal removed, and how?

I knew nothing about the process, but on closer inspection noted that the kiln was raised up on thick stands, with bare earth beneath. Several thick metal poles easily ten feet long lay on the hard ground close by. Trying to figure out how the kiln worked, I picked one up and slid it under the kiln. Much to my surprise, the entire thing lifted up easily because of the long fulcrum. Lowering it, I checked out several other bizarre pieces of ironmongery.

A tripod caught my eye, which I guessed could be used to rest the pole on to keep the kiln raised up if needed. How very bizarre. And how very interesting. The chimneys were to let out the smoke, or was it steam? Was this how our mystery victim was cooked? It felt so outlandish, but also likely, but there was one major drawback to any of this making sense.

How on earth could you get the body to the campsite?

"There's got to be a proper way in and out of here.

We need to follow the path," I told Mickey and Sue when I returned.

"If it gets us out of here, then I'm all for it," said Mickey, teasing his long blond hair nervously.

"You okay?"

"Yeah, sure. This is intense," he laughed nervously. "It's like a horror story with illegal hunting and so many knives. We should scarper."

"And right now," said Sue, shuffling closer to Mickey.

"There's a path heading further east, so let's see if there are any tracks. Maybe whoever comes here uses a quad, or you can get a small car in and out."

Anxious sat, waiting patiently for whatever came next, so I bent and made a big fuss of my brave partner, telling him how brilliant he'd been and that he was the one who'd found the clues, which made him happy. He trotted along beside me as we moved onto the track.

It was wider than I'd anticipated, and easily able to fit a quad, but the ground was so hard that there was nothing but the very faintest of tire tracks which could have been ancient.

We ambled along, side by side, keeping a keen eye on the trees and glancing behind repeatedly. Soon we moved from the scrubby ground to the edge of the forest, but the track skirted the dense interior and followed an ancient fence. Most of the posts had rotted away and the wire tangled through the nettles.

Ten minutes later, I could smell smoke, and realised I'd lost my bearings and we were approaching the campsite. The faint sound of voices drifted through the trees, and yet we were still the other side of the woods.

Out in the open like this, the temperature had become almost too much to bear, and I worried for Sue's much paler skin. Even though she was tanned like Mickey, she had red arms, and I noted I was the same. Mickey was just getting browner. A rich, deep golden hue of a true surfer poster boy.

Sunlight beat down on the dry track, the dust causing everyone to sneeze, so we stepped onto the parched grass and gasped with relief when we got under the shade of the trees.

A blinding light startled me and I put up a hand for the others to stop as I crept forward, almost laughing with relief when I realised it was no insane stalker hiding in the trees ready to end our lives, but a wing mirror.

"Guys, can you give me a hand?" I asked, dragging a branch away.

"What have you found?" asked Mickey, a sudden renewed sense of enthusiasm sparking interest behind his kind blue eyes.

"A vehicle. A motorbike maybe?"

We pulled off branches and ivy to uncover a sight I hadn't seen in a long time.

"A motorbike and sidecar! So cool," gushed Mickey.

"Why is it hidden?" asked Sue, stepping back and checking for killers. "Why not park it somewhere properly?"

"Because you don't want it to be found. Right, Max?" Mickey grinned as he reached out before yanking his hand away. "Guess the cops will want to check for fingerprints. Wonder whose it is?"

"The killer's?" I suggested, eyebrows raised.

"Or someone who likes bombing about the countryside," suggested Sue. "Although you'd want a scrambler, not this old thing."

"Old thing?" admonished Mickey with a wag of his finger. "This is a classic. Look at it. It's so cool. I'd love to ride in a sidecar. Bet it's awesome."

"It's looking like we know how this was done," I said, although something still nagged at me. Maybe just the strangeness of it all, as though we'd gone back in time to a different way of life where people hunted for food, made their own charcoal, and rode around on ancient motorbikes with sidecars.

That was it! What was bugging me. Why a sidecar? Why this antique machine rather than a modern quad bike?

For an accomplice? Or to transport the meat and other items to and from the shack?

With the bike and sidecar uncovered, we stood back and admired what was, admittedly, a fine-looking vehicle. I knew nothing about them, but Mickey thought it was midsixties judging by the style, but there was nothing to tell us about the owner, and the sidecar was empty, not even a helmet.

But just because we couldn't see something, didn't mean those smaller than us with highly sensitive noses couldn't discover more. Anxious sniffed around the vehicle, then focused on the sidecar. With a high-pitched yip, he sprang into the seat and began licking at the leather. My stomach turned, as did he have the taste of meat? Had this been used to transport a human corpse?

I lifted him out and asked him to leave it alone, then set him down. Something sprang from the trees, causing everyone to jump a mile, and he was off, tearing after a rabbit as surprised as us to discover it had company.

"Let's get back to camp," insisted Sue, sweating and red.

"Good idea," agreed Mickey. "You're burning up, babe. We need to get you cooled down."

Gratefully, we skirted the treeline, the buzz of the campsite getting louder, then took a path into welcome deep shade. A few minutes later, with Anxious having given up the chase and now tearing after us, we emerged a short distance from Dan's tent into a world that felt utterly strange after such a macabre hour or so.

The campsite was still awash with all manner of busy and important people. Detectives, constables, teams at the tent, and a large contingent of firefighters.

What was missing, though, were the guests.

It was hardly surprising. I assumed that after the

terrible night everyone suffered they'd cleared out the moment the police said they could. All that remained was Vee, the pink metal box of misery, and Mickey and Sue's VW.

"Everyone's gone," lamented Sue. "How sad."

"You can't blame them," said Mickey. "People were poorly, or scared, and with a second murder and the house burning down, everyone's super jittery."

"But we're still here," whispered Sue, like she couldn't quite believe it.

"Maybe it's best if we leave," said Mickey, looking to Sue for her reaction.

"No!" she growled, stamping her foot. "We're going to help Max figure this out. You are, Mickey. You wanted an adventure, to be involved in a real mystery, and now you have one."

"But it might be dangerous," he said.

"If we stick together, nothing will happen. You look after me, I look after you."

"Always," he said, nodding vigorously then kissing her cheek.

Anxious ran off, barking loudly to tell Mum and Dad he was back, and for them to get the cuddles ready, while the three of us arranged to meet later. First, we had to tell the detectives what we'd uncovered. We met them halfway across the field. Both appeared distracted and exhausted.

"Busy time?" I asked.

"Yes, but it's not the official work that's so draining," grumbled Sherry.

"No, it's them." Liam pointed to Mum and Dad, who waved happily; Anxious was in Dad's lap having his tummy rubbed.

"Ah," I said knowingly. "They cornered you and started talking, then an hour later you realised you'd hardly said a word but knew a lot more about the nineteen-fifties than you did before."

"They do like to talk," said Sherry. "They're nice people, but there's only so much tea you can drink and only so many times you tell someone you can't discuss a case before you start to go funny in the head. Where have you been?"

We explained what we'd found, and their eyes lit up, eager to get going and investigate. I excused myself for a moment to let the two remaining happy campers know I had to leave again for a while, then returned. Mickey and Sue remained at their van, clearly overwhelmed and preferring to leave me to retrace the route we'd just taken.

Teams were called to process the scenes, the bike left in place and the shack swarmed with specialists that were wrapping up at the campsite. I kept my opinions to myself, mostly because I was utterly exhausted now, and more than anything I just wanted to rest.

Once I'd shown them everything we'd found, I returned alone to the campsite and the glorious, utterly welcome site of three of the four souls I loved most in the world fast asleep. Anxious was upside down on Dad's lap, head lolling, legs akimbo, and Mum and Dad were holding hands while they snored, their heads back, mouths open.

I practically crawled into Vee, wrangled with the bed, turned on the fan, and was asleep before my head hit the pillow.

Chapter 16

I woke up to a sweaty mess. It took a heartbeat to realise I was the sweaty mess. The fan had clicked off for some reason and it was stifling in the van, so I clambered out, blinded by the sun.

Maybe it was the shock, maybe it was everything we'd discovered that morning, or maybe because my mind was utterly empty, but I had what I could only describe as an epiphany.

Where before there had been faint suspicion, now there was certainty. I frowned as I stood hunched over in the doorway of my home, wondering if I was delusional because of the heat and exhaustion, but all I felt was sure.

The motorbike, the shack, and everything else that had happened now had me convinced I knew exactly what'd been going on around here. All that remained was to prove it.

I nipped back inside and got a cool drink of lemonade from the fridge. Usually reserved for Min, I'd become addicted to them and knew I had to break the habit, but needed something cold and fizzy. It was either that or Prosecco, so I took the lesser of two evils.

Sitting on the step, I glanced around the now almost deserted campsite. Mickey and Sue were relaxing under their shun shelter and waved happily when they spied me, so I waved back then smiled as a sense of smugness washed over me, causing a little guilt as this was nothing to feel good about.

There was nobody else around. The police had left, the vehicles were gone, and with the other holidaymakers having vanished the site was looking sad. Patches of yellow grass where tents had been pitched were a stark reminder that things were not right at this otherwise beautiful location. People wanted to have a nice time and a relaxing few days, but sometimes life slaps you across the head rather than kisses you on the lips, and I guessed some campsites were just better than others.

Wondering where the fifties fanatics and Anxious were, I didn't have long to wait until I got my answer. They came from the direction of the house with Joni in tow, either very reluctantly or just too shell-shocked to consider turning down what I just knew was Mum's offer of tea and sympathy.

Anxious led the way, head held high, like he was leading a procession rather than a poor woman who'd lost everything in the span of a few hours. I washed my face hurriedly, applied deodorant, then put the kettle on.

"Look who we found, love," squealed Mum like Joni was a long-lost bestie.

"Poor thing's half dead, excuse the language," said Dad with a smile.

"How are you doing, Joni?" I asked, sorting out mugs.

"About as well as can be expected. Max, everyone's gone."

"I know. I'm sorry. Sugar and milk?"

"Two sugars and a splash of milk. Thank you."

I continued making tea while I asked, "What did the police say?"

"That they'll most likely be back at some point, but have everything they need for now."

"Which is?"

"Absolutely nothing as far as I can tell. They only left a few minutes ago as the detectives explained what you found and asked me a lot of questions about it."

"Yes, I suspected they might. Joni, why didn't you tell them?"

"What's this?" asked Dad, sitting on the edge of his seat.

I quickly filled them in on what we'd discovered, then asked Joni again, "Why hadn't you told them about it earlier?"

"Why do you think?"

"Because Dan warned you not to?"

"Exactly. He's always been a hunter. He adored the outdoors life and was that way since a little boy. He used to hunt with his father and tried to get our Mike involved, but he was never very trustworthy with a weapon." Joni laughed weakly. "Lad couldn't get the hang of it and refused to shoot an animal."

"That's fair enough."

"Yes, of course. But Dan loved to hunt, and he always used the shack."

"You used the meat for the business, didn't you?" I asked, knowing the answer.

"Yes. Max, it's always been a struggle to stay afloat here. We don't get the custom, and everything keeps going up in price. Utilities, all the food, it's impossible to manage. So Dan would hunt, and we used what he caught to keep costs down."

"Was my chop even pork?" growled Dad.

"Dad, it was pork."

"But for the pies, and other things, we used Dan's hunting skills to keep the business going."

"You kept it from the police as you knew you'd get shut down and he'd be in serious trouble for illegal hunting," I said.

"Of course. I didn't think it would matter. It was just hunting. Nothing to do with the body that was found in the caravan."

"What about the bike? Why was it hidden like that? Why didn't he just park it at the car park?"

"Dan was always very cautious about his hunting, and insisted on keeping the bike hidden then carrying the meat in the back way so nobody would ever suspect him. He's had that motorbike and sidecar for as long as I've known him. It was his grandfather's, so meant a lot to him. He used to spend hours tinkering with it. I think he loved it more than he loved me. In fact, I know he did." Joni's head shot up and she locked her eyes on mine as she admitted, "Most of the time, we didn't get on. We were never very happy, but I didn't know what else to do. Is that awful?"

"No, just rather sad," I said.

"It isn't your fault, love," said Mum, taking the chance to give Joni a quick hug. "Marriage is hard for some people."

"And now he's dead and my home and business, is gone. Everything's gone."

"Joni, I don't know if the detectives asked you this, but I'd like you to tell me the truth. Of course, you don't have to, but you asked for my help and I'm going to keep to my word. Did Dan hunt alone, or did he sometimes go with someone else? Before you answer, please think carefully about what you say. I only ask because I don't believe Dan used the kiln alone, although please correct me if I'm wrong."

"Sometimes," she said cautiously. "Why do you ask?" I waited, then the penny finally dropped. "Oh no! You don't think that's who was in the caravan, do you? I never even gave it a thought. Neither did Dan. They weren't best friends or anything like that, but they went back a long way to when they were younger and their dads used to hunt with them. Yes, he hunted with his friend sometimes and it was him who usually did the charcoal, although Dan got good at it, too, the last few years."

"But neither of you thought to mention it to the police or to check on him?"

"Why would we? They often went weeks or months between seeing each other. The charcoal wasn't made often, and they only hunted together a few times a year. I never even considered it might be Carl who was killed."

"Are we saying Dan killed him?" asked Dad.

"Dan's dead, remember?" said Mum, patting Dad's head like was getting forgetful.

"I know that!" He batted Mum's hand away, then smoothed back his hair. "He might have killed this Carl fellow before then."

"So who killed Dan?" asked Mum.

"That's a very good question," I said.

"This is too much. I don't know what to think about anything. I need to go." Joni stopped suddenly, causing Anxious to snap awake then settle once he realised there was no danger.

"What about your tea?" asked Mum. "And where are you going anyway? Your house burned down, remember?"

"Mum, she knows that."

We watched Joni hurry across the field, glancing quickly at Dan's tent, the crime scene tape still in place. She shuddered before she broke into a run and was soon gone.

"You prat," sighed Dad. "Of course she knows her house burned down."

"Don't you call me that. That's swearing, that is," scowled Mum.

"It's not swearing. It's a small fish."

"Then don't you call me a small fish!" huffed Mum.

Ignoring her, Dad turned to me and asked, "So what are we thinking? This Carl fella is dead and that was him in the caravan? Poor guy. Dan offed him and Joni knew about it, so helped cover up the murder?"

Mum tutted. "Now who's the prat? If that happened,

who killed Dan and burned the house down?"

"The son, maybe?"

"He definitely had a grudge against his dad. But he wouldn't burn his own house down. No, there's a killer on the loose somewhere," said Mum with a shudder.

"Most likely, Carl is the victim. I'll call the detectives and they can check on him. Maybe he's fine and it was someone else."

"But why dump him in our caravan?" asked Dad. "It's so dumb. You don't hide a murder that way."

"Unless…" I began.

"Guys, what's the latest?" asked Mickey as he ambled over, grinning, seemingly ready to get back in the game. He took in our faces and asked, "Sorry, am I interrupting? I saw Joni leave and wanted to catch up on anything I'd missed. My bad." With a shrug, Mickey turned to leave.

"Hey, it's fine. Mickey, come and join us. Let me fill you in on what Joni said. Then I really need to make a call." After explaining, Mickey was almost beside himself with excitement.

"So we're saying Dan killed this Carl dude, but then someone killed him? Is that it?"

"Not quite, no. Let's not speculate yet, as there's still plenty to uncover, but I was just about to tell Mum and Dad that I'm convinced the killer wanted the body to be found."

"It's certainly made for an interesting few days," grinned Mickey.

"Hasn't it been the best?" gushed Mum. "Apart from the food poisoning and killings, of course. But it's been fun to have a real life case to solve. I feel like Miss Marple."

"More like Miss Carpal," said Dad, chortling at his own "joke."

"What's that supposed to mean?" snapped Mum, flexing her fingers.

"Because you have damaged nerves in your hand.

Carpal tunnel syndrome. That's what you have, isn't it?"

"What if I do?" she hissed.

"Anyway," I interrupted, knowing they'd bicker for ages otherwise, "as I was saying. It's likely that the killer wanted the body found."

"Stands to reason. Otherwise, why put it in a bright pink caravan?" Mickey winced as he glanced at the looming beast.

"Exactly. But I do need to call the detectives." I wandered into the field, no chance of interrupting a game of football now, and called Sherry. She said she'd be in touch, and thanked me, then asked the obvious, like his surname, where he lived, or his phone number. When I admitted I didn't know, she tutted, and chastised me for overlooking such basic information, but said she'd call Joni.

I felt rather ashamed after hanging up, reminding myself that I still had plenty to learn about investigating crimes and I should be more mindful and not assume everything was going to get worked out without putting in the time and effort. But then I laughed because I also had to remind myself that I wasn't a detective. I was a vanlifer with an unsettling knack for getting into the thick of things.

I'd hardly had time to finish my tea before the two detectives arrived. They were certainly keen, and I was surprised they'd shown up, but offered them a drink.

Mum and Dad fired off the usual questions, and they answered politely but were clearly keen to have a word in private, so we excused ourselves and walked towards the house.

"We can't find Joni," said Sherry. "I spoke to her on the phone and she gave me Carl's details, but now she's vanished. Any ideas?"

"No, none. With her son, or a friend? I don't know where she's been today. I met her at the campsite."

"We'll keep calling, but figured we should come in person. Max, we found out about this Carl and went around to his house. He wasn't there, but we spoke to a neighbour and he hasn't been back for a few days. It ties in with the time of death of the deceased, and we dug up photos on social media. Of course, we need someone to confirm his identity, and the bods back at the office are digging up his family, excuse the poor choice of words, so it shouldn't take long."

"But it's him, right?"

"Looks that way. What's worrying is that Joni kept it quiet. Dan too."

"They were concerned about his hunting being discovered, but I think Joni was telling the truth and hadn't even considered it being Dan's buddy. Like she said, why would she?"

"Because a stewed, cooked, steamed, whatever you want to describe it as, corpse was found on their property. They should have checked on everyone they knew," said Liam, smiling.

"To be fair, that's not what people do, is it?" said Sherry. "We have to remember, we're professionals. The general population doesn't automatically assume they know who's been murdered in such a bizarre way."

"Still seems suspect to me," said Liam.

"I'm sure it was a genuine oversight. But look, I'm glad you came. I wanted to talk to you again anyway. I'm sure everything's come together now, and if we approach this the right way we should have everything tied up soon."

"Do tell?" said Sherry with a wink at Liam. "See, I told you he was good. Now, let's hear what you have to say, Max. And spare no details."

Once I'd gone over my reasoning, and why I believed what I did, not even skipping my epiphany when I stumbled from the van after a nap, neither said a word.

Then they both burst out laughing and high-fived before turning to me, hands raised, and I reluctantly returned the gesture. They beamed at me, and I simply couldn't figure these two out. Muscular, tanned, healthy, wearing workout clothes and worryingly clean Nikes, they were incongruous and the antithesis of beaten-down detectives. But it wasn't even their fitness fanaticism, it was their seeming utter lack of stress.

"Doesn't this phase you? Don't you get overworked and stressed-out? Tired of what you see and how hard you work?"

"He's still not sure about us," Sherry told Liam.

"Thinks were hiding things."

"Maybe we are," laughed Sherry.

"Maybe."

"Max, you need to chill. Like we told you, we don't get many murders, and we take this job in our stride. It's work we love, but there's life, too, you know? Stuff to enjoy. Things to do. Books to read, movies to watch, and games to play. We've found the work life balance. Everyone thinks the same as you, but the simple truth is that we don't take our work home with us and do proper policing while we're on the clock."

"That makes perfect sense. Now what do you think about my ideas?"

"We think you need to stop showing us up and solving multiple murders and arson before we do," said Liam with a wicked grin. "Nah, it's all good. Let us look into things discreetly, and we still need to find Joni, but yes, you're probably correct. This life never ceases to surprise you, does it?" Liam shook his head, his smile faltering for once.

"That's what makes it worth living," said Sherry. "See you, Max." With a cheery wave, they headed back towards the house.

"What's the deal, Son?" asked Dad as he appeared with Anxious.

"I told them what I believe happened, and they agree. At least I think they do. It's hard to tell with those two. And they can't find Joni."

"Did they trace this Carl guy?"

"He hasn't been home for a few days. It's him, most likely."

"So it was Dan who killed him?" Dad nodded sagely.

"I doubt it. Let's get back to Mum and I'll explain everything. Then we should try to find Joni."

"Sure, whatever you think is best. But don't you go taking all the credit. Let your mother have some of the glory for this. It'll make her feel better about herself." Dad winked and I nodded.

After telling Mum about Carl, I finally managed to explain my theory without any interruptions. Or at least part of it. I had to hold a few things back as otherwise I knew this could go very wrong, very quickly.

"Well I never," gasped Mum when I'd finished.

"He's a smart lad," said Dad, nodding his approval, love in his eyes.

"I don't know about that. Everything seemed to click into place earlier, and chatting to everyone today confirmed what I already knew. Now comes the hard part. Proving it."

"We have to be sneaky and get them to admit it." Mum rubbed her hands together, eyes unfocused.

I glanced at Dad and we exchanged a smile, then I asked her, "Any ideas? How do you go about getting someone to admit something like this?"

"You leave that to me. You might be the best at figuring out seemingly impossible mysteries, but the one thing I'm great at is getting people to talk."

"When you let them get a word in edgeways," said Dad. "You can't stop nattering."

"I do not natter. I talk only when it's appropriate to do so." Even Mum couldn't keep a straight face and we laughed before I reluctantly got together something for lunch. Nobody was particularly hungry, but we had to eat, as none of us knew how long it might be before we got another chance.

Regardless, after missing an evening meal yesterday and having to endure the results, I not only whipped us up a nice chicken salad for lunch, but prepared dinner after we'd eaten. Tonight would be something that we loved more than just about any other dish. Simple, delicious, and with a few secret ingredients that made it unbeatable. Good old beef stew.

Once it was simmering away, and would continue to do so for the rest of the day before I'd turn the heat off and let it continue to cook under its own steam, I went for a long walk with Anxious back into the town to pick up some crusty bread. You can't have beef stew without something suitably artisan to soak up the incredible gravy, and my parents would most likely disown me if there wasn't bread.

Chapter 17

With a lovely loaf in my bag for life, I whistled as I walked back to the campsite along a country lane, not surprised to be stopped halfway home by Joni.

"Fancy a lift?" she asked, hope in her eyes. "I could do with the company."

"As long as you don't mind dogs, then I'd love one."

"Of course. Both of you hop in."

Anxious didn't need telling twice, so the moment I opened the door of the small white van he jumped in and settled in the middle of the bench style seat. After buckling up, I patted my lap but he was seemingly happy where he was and curled up with a groan.

"Poor guy's shattered," I explained.

"Aren't we all?" Joni sped off, anticipating the turns expertly after having driven them countless times over the years.

"The police were looking for you. The detectives said they spoke to you, but then they couldn't get an answer again and you weren't at the campsite."

"I didn't want to hear any more bad news. I needed time to myself. This is a lot to deal with. Dan's gone, the house, too, and I just don't know what I'm going to do."

"I understand. Hey, are those the keys for the

motorbike and sidecar?" I asked, reaching forward and retrieving a set of keys from the bay behind the gear stick.

Joni glanced down then shrugged, eyes back on the road. "I guess. There are a few sets hanging around. He should have got rid of the stupid thing years ago, but Dan was sentimental in some ways."

"It was part of his heritage. And it is a very cool vehicle. You ever ride in it?"

"Many years ago, but once he started using it for the meat, not so much."

"Makes sense. What are you going to do now?"

"Check things at the house. See if there's anything to salvage. I couldn't bear to look for long earlier, but now Dan's been taken away and the fire's out properly, I want to see."

"I'm sorry this happened, Joni. Truly. It's been a terrible time."

"Thank you. But I appreciate you sticking around and trying to figure things out. Have you got anywhere? I know we think it was Carl, but what about my Dan?"

"Things are still very confusing, but I'm sure once it's confirmed it was Carl, everything else will fall into place."

"How so?" she turned to me then away as we came to a bend.

"Call it a hunch, call it how these things work out, but the end is in sight."

Joni pulled into the car park, avoiding looking at the house, then parked and killed the engine. For a moment she said nothing, just clasped her hands in her lap, then she whispered, "All I want is for this to be over." Without another word, she got out.

"What do you think, Anxious? Is it nearly over? I think it is."

Anxious sat up and grunted, but his eyes were almost closed again. It was time to finish this, and time to move on. But not before a good night's sleep and a rather dramatic prelude.

On my way back to the camper, I stopped at Mickey and Sue's.

"How are you both doing? Your colour's eased off," I said, turning to Sue.

"We're okay. I put some cream on and stayed in the shade and the redness has gone down. Yours too. I thought both our arms were going to get burned."

"I'm fine," beamed Mickey, flexing his biceps.

"You never burn. You just get more tanned," noted Sue.

"Guys, if you're up for it, I want to go back to the cabin and take another look. And at the bike. What do you say?"

"I'm feeling totally shattered," sighed Sue. "It's a long walk, and what will we find? It's just that old shack and that horrible meat."

"Come on, babe, it'll be fun. We're finally involved in a murder mystery and it's so cool." Mickey hopped from one foot to another, keen to start.

"For you, anything." Sue smiled sweetly as Mickey pulled her in for a squeeze.

"Yes!"

"Come over in five and we'll head off?"

"Sure. We'll be there," agreed Mickey.

I returned to the camper with Anxious trotting along happily, dropped off the bread, then explained to the two eager sleuths what the plan was. They tried their best to act normal, but both were beside themselves with excitement and kept glancing around, making it utterly obvious they had a secret.

"Cool it," I sighed. "Act natural and stop grinning."

"We are cool," said Dad, running his steel comb through his hair.

"As cucumbers," agreed Mum, slipping into her

trainers, never mind she was wearing a black, flared dress with hundreds of red dots and a neckline so low I didn't know where to look.

"Good. I'll be back in a few minutes, so sit tight and don't do anything daft."

"Like what?" asked Dad.

"I'm not about to tell you. If I do, you'll probably do it."

"Smart boy," trilled Mum happily.

Shaking my head, but unable to stop my smile spreading, I crossed the campsite once more, took the path, crunched over the gravel car park, then approached the front of the house.

The walls were black above the windows where the fire had licked up the stonework; all the windows were smashed.

The thatched roof was gone, exposing rafters that creaked and groaned as the house settled after the damage.

Joni emerged as I got to the front door, looking even smaller than usual. Her slender frame was shaking, and as she brushed limp black hair from sunken eyes she smudged soot all over her face. Her hands were filthy.

"It's all gone," she confirmed as our eyes met. "The place is a total write-off. The fire department said it was, that there wasn't much left, and the building isn't structurally sound now, but I had to see for myself."

"You need to be careful. It might collapse. Nothing in there is worth risking your life over." After guiding her down the steps, I let go of her hand, more like a child's than a grown woman's, and asked, "Did you get anything? You didn't go upstairs, did you?"

"I couldn't get up there. The staircase is half gone. I found a few things in the back room. Just little trinkets. A dumb ornament that means nothing, and a few pairs of shoes. I couldn't even be bothered to take them."

"Best to stay away now. Leave it to the insurance

company to deal with. They might get it fixed. Did you call them?"

"Yes. The police gave me an incident number so I called. I don't know when they'll come, or even if they'll cover the damage. But I think I'm done with this place now. Too many memories, and most of them not good. Of course, some are wonderful, especially when Mike was a baby, but that feels like a different life now."

"We're going to return to the shack. See if this terrible thing can finally be resolved. Will you come? I know it's hard, but you might be able to help. Did the detectives call you and ask?"

"They already called. I don't know if I can. What am I supposed to say? That my husband was an illegal hunter, we sold meat we weren't allowed to, his friend is dead, and I kept quiet about his hunting for fear of getting into trouble when it meant I stopped you figuring things out sooner?"

"Joni, it's alright. You didn't know it was Carl who was found in the caravan. That's understandable. I know this is hard, but it might help you accept what's happened."

"How?" Joni smeared more soot over her face as she rubbed at her cheeks as though waking from a dream.

"I'm not sure," I admitted. "But come anyway. The police need you there to confirm a few things, so you'll have to do it at some point. Might as well be now."

"Okay."

"Maybe go and wash up first, then come over to ours and we'll be off."

"I don't even have a bathroom. I'll have to use the campsite one."

"At least you keep it nice and clean. It is a stunning spot you have here."

"Then make the most of it, because you're the very last guest to stay here."

Joni was silent as we returned to the campsite, then plodded numbly to the bathroom while I returned to the others.

Things were slotting into place, and it wouldn't be long now.

"Are you ready for this?" I asked Anxious as he trotted alongside without a care in the world.

A happy yip was my answer.

I chuckled despite the seriousness of the situation. "Good, because I want you to stay close and if I need you, please do what you do best."

Anxious sat and cocked his head, then licked his lips.

"No, not eat biscuits." I stifled a smile as his ears pricked up at the word. "Although you do a fine job of that. I mean, bite ankles."

My faithful pooch looked around, as if there was one ready and waiting to attack, then turned back to me.

"Fine, you can have a biscuit now. But stay close." I handed over a small treat, which he took in his usual gentle manner, then crunched happily before we got to the campervan. Mum and Dad were ready, and Mickey and Sue arrived a moment later.

Joni emerged from the bathroom block tugging her hair into a ponytail, then slowly walked over, her hands clasped like she was heading a funeral procession.

"Joni, how are you holding up?" asked Mickey with sympathy. "I'm so sorry about Dan and the property. Shouldn't you be lying down or, er, doing funeral stuff?"

"I don't know what I should be doing, but I can't arrange a funeral today. Dan only died this morning."

"Yeah, right, sorry." Mickey nodded, then brightened as he asked, "Are you coming to the shack? Pretty cool, eh? I mean, not cool you were selling dodgy meat to customers, but at least we know who the guy in the caravan was. It's coming together."

"Yes, I suppose it is."

Sue nudged Mickey and shook her head. Mickey

frowned in confusion, oblivious to his rather insensitive remarks.

Anxious led the way to the far end of the campsite, past Dan's tent, which everyone avoided commenting on, then into the woods and along the well-worn path. It didn't take long to emerge the other side of this narrow strip, to discover the motorbike and sidecar still in place.

"He really loved that old machine," said Joni after a quick glance.

"Now that is a very fine piece of machinery," gushed Dad as he hurried over and stroked the handlebars. "Proper classic. Bet your Dan loved this, eh?" he asked Joni.

"He adored it. But riding in a sidecar is utterly terrifying."

"Maybe we should get one?" Dad suggested to Mum. "We could go for trips."

"I am not getting in something like that! How would I even fit with my dress?"

"You could wear jeans," suggested Mickey.

My parents gawped at Mickey like he'd suggested she go in her knickers.

"Are you mad, son?" spluttered Dad.

Mum's mouth opened and closed, but no words escaped. Miracle of miracles.

"Look what you've done to my wife! I think you broke her." Dad glared at Mickey who shrank in on himself under the ferocity of his glare.

"I... I was just saying she could wear jeans."

Mum's legs buckled and Dad had to grab her quick before she collapsed.

"Mum doesn't do jeans," I told Mickey.

"Course she doesn't," snapped Dad. "She's a lady of a certain style, and you better take that back, lad, before she clobbers you."

"Um, yeah, sure. Sorry." Mickey shrugged, utterly out of his depth.

"Can we please get on?" asked Joni. "I just want to go and lie down somewhere. Will everyone stop with this nonsense? Jack, if you want the motorbike and sidecar, it's yours."

"You mean it?" he asked, forgetting about Mum and releasing her.

"Absolutely. I always hated the thing, and I doubt it will ever be used again. I don't even want to sell it. It's yours."

"Awesome! You hear that, Jill? It's ours."

"I told you, I am not getting in that thing."

They continued their bickering as we made our way along the track, Anxious ensuring he remained by my side in case ankles needed biting or there was a surprise attack from the woods.

As we closed in on the shack, low voices carried on the stifling breeze, and Joni stopped. "There are people here?"

"Just the detectives, remember? You spoke to them and they said they would check out the shack again. It's already been gone over by other teams, but they wanted more time. It's best we help them out now before even more specialists arrive and the area is swamped. If Carl used to come here with Dan, they'll want to check absolutely everything. You okay? It isn't too much for you?"

"No, I'm hanging in there, and you're right. Best to get this over with now."

I increased my pace, and everyone hurried to catch up, and soon enough we emerged into the ramshackle clearing Dan and his buddy had used for their hunting and charcoal making.

Approaching from a different angle, it confirmed for me that this was a very well-hidden spot, although when they made charcoal I was sure the smoke could have been seen for miles. But who would think anything of it? Surrounded by farms and country houses, fires were always being lit at all times of the year.

I assumed that was very infrequent anyway, and their main work of hunting and butchering the animals here made it the perfect, private location.

"You okay?" I asked Joni as she paused.

"Yes. Let's make this quick."

"What about you, babe?" Mickey asked Sue.

"Just tired. I don't like this place. It's like a horror movie. Look at all the hooks!"

"They're only bits of metal. Nothing to worry about. And we're here with you. Maybe we'll figure something out."

"Maybe, but I don't want to stay long. You've helped a lot already, Mickey. I'm very proud of you."

Mickey beamed with pride as Sue kissed his cheek, but when she glanced at the shack her expression changed. As she shifted away from him and studied the kiln, I knew exactly what had gone on here.

"Hi. How you folks doing this fine afternoon?" asked Liam as he and Sherry approached, removing their gloves as they stopped before us.

"Lovely day for it," said Sherry with a wink.

"Is it?" snapped Joni. "My husband was murdered, my house burned down, I expect I'm in trouble for not realising the body was Carl, and you're saying it's a lovely day?"

"Merely a figure of speech, ma'am," said Liam, his smile unfaltering. "Shall we get on?" he asked, turning to me.

"I think we better.

"Get on?" asked Joni. "What's this really about?"

"Isn't it obvious?" asked Sherry with a broad smile. "Max is about to reveal the murderer." She turned to Liam and said, "I can't wait for this. I've never done a big reveal before. It's exciting."

"Will you stop acting so happy!" shouted Joni, tugging at her ponytail. "Go on then, tell us," she spat, whipping around to confront me.

I took a deep breath, stood back a little so everyone was facing me, and said, "Sue put the body of Carl in the caravan."

Mickey's smile wavered then fell as he turned to Sue. She was deathly pale and looked ready to run.

But then she sighed deeply, nodded, and told Mickey, "I'm so sorry. Things got out of hand and I didn't know what to do. I'm so sorry."

Chapter 18

Mickey laughed as he looked from Sue to me then back again. "Very funny! You nearly had me going for a moment there. As if Sue could kill a guy and put him in a caravan."

"I thought you'd ask Max to get involved and help solve the case," wailed Sue, tears streaming down her blotchy face.

"Babe, you kept saying how you hated all the talk of murders and that I was becoming obsessed. I wouldn't then go and get involved, now would I?" Mickey shrugged, looking entirely out of place with his faded denim shorts and no shirt when talking about what Sue'd done to cheer him up. "And besides, you guys are teasing, right? Although, it's in bad taste what with Joni here having lost her husband."

"Son, you better listen to the girl," said Dad softly.

Mickey's smile faltered as the truth dawned on him. "You killed this Carl guy?"

"No, of course not," sniffled Sue, wiping her eyes.

"So it is a joke?" he asked, confused.

"She found the body, I assume," I said. "Sue, I'm guessing you discovered Carl by accident? You've been here alone before, haven't you? You came up with a plan to make Mickey happy?"

"Yes! Yes, that's it. Mickey, you kept talking about Max, and how you wished you could be involved in things like him. I was walking the other day and came across this place. The man, Carl, although I had no idea who he was, gave me the shock of my life when I found him in the charcoal kiln."

"You can confirm he was already dead?" asked Liam.

"Yes, I would never kill someone. He was dead. Something must have gone wrong with the charcoal making. I wasn't sure. He was inside, and just laying there. I didn't know what to do. The ladder was right beside the kiln, so I guess he'd climbed up to look inside but fell in. Maybe trying to remove the lids? I ran back towards the campsite, but something went funny in my head and I thought what if I could leave everything and let Mickey discover the body with Max. Then they could solve the case together."

"So why didn't you?" asked Sherry. "Or better yet, call it in."

"I knew Mickey would love the intrigue. When I discovered the motorbike, I decided to see if I could get it started. I found the keys in the shack. I drove it back here and managed to lever the kiln up enough to pull Carl out. I got caught up in what felt like a silly game, and didn't expect to get him out, but the pole made it easy and he just slid out on a tarp I put down. Then I dragged him into the sidecar."

"But he was naked," protested Mickey. "And why on earth would he be inside the kiln? How could he fall in? This makes no sense."

"It probably got left unattended and burned away," noted Liam. "If you don't control the airflow properly it will burn like a regular fire. Carl must have fallen when the ladder slipped, or had a heart attack possibly, and tumbled inside. I'm guessing he got knocked out, or was already dead, then baked or steamed because of the residual heat. These things get incredibly hot."

"We're still waiting on the postmortem," said Sherry, "but he had a fair few bumps and bruises. The most obvious answer is that he banged his head and that was the end of him."

"I'm so, so sorry," sobbed Sue. "I thought you'd enjoy the mystery. I knew Max's parents were coming, so rather than wait for someone to possibly find Carl, I decided to hide him in the caravan when they went for a walk." Sue turned to us and mumbled, "Sorry for the upset. I know it was ghastly. I almost gave up partway through as it was so disgusting, but I pulled him inside using the tarp then regretted it instantly. It took a lot of effort to drag him through the woods, and I was going to leave him there, but then I couldn't resist using the caravan. I even took his clothes because I worried about evidence. I'm so dumb. It was a cruel, horrid thing to do. It made me feel so sick, but I knew my Mickey would be excited about the mystery."

"That's alright, love," said Mum. "We all do daft stuff sometimes."

"Mistakes happen," shrugged Dad. "The main thing is nobody was murdered." Liam cleared his throat and Dad coughed as he said, "Oops! Sorry, Joni, I was forgetting. So, if Sue didn't kill Carl, who murdered Dan and burned down the house?"

"No, wait just one minute!" demanded Mickey. "Sue, babe, you know I love you more than anything, but you did this for me? You found a corpse, loaded it into a sidecar, and hid the guy in a bright pink caravan? And all for me?"

"Yes." Sue's head lifted and she met Mickey's gleaming eyes.

"That is so awesome! Thanks, babe." Mickey picked Sue up and twirled her around.

"You aren't cross?" she asked, as bewildered as everyone else.

"Cross? Well, yeah, I guess." Mickey scratched his head, still smiling. "But that's true love, that is. You knew I wanted to help solve a mystery, so you gave me one. But, um, will Sue go to prison?" he asked Liam and Sherry.

They nodded to each other, then Sherry said, "Most likely she'll get a record, and there will be harsh penalties, but no prison, no. She interfered with a crime scene, but as far as we're aware, there was no murder committed. Or if there was, Dan did it, and he's not telling."

"You hear that?" squealed Mickey. "Babe, it will be okay."

"You don't hate me?"

"Course not. You did this for me. You're awesome. Amazing."

"Aw, aren't they sweet," cooed Mum.

"Young love," sighed Dad.

"Which brings us to Dan and the fire," I said.

"It wasn't my Sue," declared Mickey. Turning to her, worry written large across his innocent face, he cautiously asked, "It wasn't, was it?"

"Murder? No way! Mickey, you know I'd never do that."

"Time to own up, Joni," I said sadly.

"I don't know what you're talking about! What is this?"

"You know."

"I do not, and I won't stand here and listen to another word. You've already done enough and this is over. Thank you for discovering the truth about Carl, but I need to go. I have something I need to do." Joni hurried off towards the woods, and for a moment nobody moved.

"What should we do?" asked Dad.

"Stop her, I should imagine," said Liam with a smile and a shrug.

"Don't you think you should do that?" I asked.

"This is your rodeo. You ride her down."

Knowing I'd better, I gave chase, but paused when Dad shouted, "Wait!"

"Not without us, you don't," admonished Mum as I found her and Dad right beside me.

"Can I come too?" asked Mickey.

"Why not?" I sighed. "The more the merrier. But she is getting away."

"Chill, Max," said Sherry. "Where's she going to go? She'll never make it back to the house, and if she does, about a hundred coppers are already there."

"Fair enough, but you're forgetting one thing."

"And what's that?"

"The motorbike."

"Damn!"

Sherry and Liam exchanged a look, then we hurried after the retreating figure of Joni. She was surprisingly fast, easily distancing herself from us, so I told Anxious to go bite some ankles and he tore off after her, yipping for joy as he went.

"This is so exciting," panted Mum. "Like cops and robbers, but with a nice sunny day."

"Don't they have nice weather?" asked Dad.

"Never. On the TV, it's always grim and raining when they catch the baddies. This is much nicer."

Fit because of their endless dancing, they easily kept pace with me even though I was much taller, and the detectives were a sight to behold as they raced ahead. Mickey and Sue brought up the rear, no slouches themselves, and we were soon running as a team, although I was sure the detectives slowed because they didn't want to spoil things for us.

Rounding the bend, everyone put on a burst of speed as we spied Joni up ahead. She'd slowed, and glanced behind—a fatal mistake—so stumbled, then righted and tore across the grass towards the trees.

Flashing lights strobed through the forest, and she paused, clearly undecided on her next course of action, then jumped onto the motorbike and started it with a splutter of belching fumes.

Revving manically, she skidded off the grass, tyres spitting lumps of sod at us, then stalled.

"Go get her, Anxious!" I shouted above the roar of the engine as she started the bike again and raced away.

Barking happily, Anxious sprinted after his quarry like a bullet, a blur of white and brown, determined not to miss out on a biscuit and possibly a medal.

Joni was clearly no expert biker and had hardly got up any speed when Anxious reached her. Without pausing, he leaped and landed in the sidecar, ears flapping as they rounded the bend.

Fearing for his safety, as he had neither a helmet nor goggles on, and I doubted there was even a seat belt, I redoubled my efforts, shaking my head and laughing at the realisation I was actually giving it "Max Effort." I knew my folks would be thinking the same thing, but without getting the irony, as I took the lead.

Careening through the trees, I followed the rumble of the bike and Anxious' barking and soon emerged into the campsite. Joni was already across the field and heading for the exit, but police cars were everywhere and I couldn't see how she could get through. She clearly had the same thought, and skidded to a halt then turned and drove towards me, her speed increasing as she revved the throttle.

"Anxious, here's your biscuit!" I shouted.

His head whipped around as I threw the biscuit to Joni's left, the opposite side to him, and with his mind on one thing, and one thing only, Anxious leapt from his seat, onto the handlebars, then launched into the air, snaffled the biscuit, and landed with an expert tuck and roll before sitting happily and munching on his prize.

Confused, and with the handlebars turned, Joni over-corrected, causing the sidecar to tilt, then leave the ground, before she screamed as the whole thing toppled over and she was flung free.

Rolling several times, she came to a stop, scrambled

to her feet, and was about to run off before my joyous pooch leaped into action, grabbed her trouser leg, and began growling as he tugged her back towards us. Being a slight woman, she didn't stand a chance. Anxious was stronger than he looked, especially if another treat was involved, and she ended up by my side before I handed over the little guy's prize. I congratulated him, and he released Joni as Sherry and Liam took an arm each and beamed at me.

"Sweet skills," said Sherry, laughing.

"That dog is amazing," gushed Liam.

"My Max was incredible too," said Mum, barging past Dad and smiling.

"Thanks," I grunted, then turned to Joni. "You could have got yourself killed. What were you thinking?"

"I wasn't. I just had to get away. Why did you have to spoil everything? He deserved it. He was horrible to me and my darling Mike, and never made us feel good. Now he's dead."

"So you did kill your husband?" asked Mum, slow to get up to speed with things.

"Yes! Aren't you following?" snapped Joni. "After Carl was found, it dawned on me I could use it as the perfect excuse. When Dan gave everyone food poisoning, it was the ideal opportunity. I killed him that night while he was snoring. He was drunk again, the pig, and I knew I'd get away with it."

"Then you burned the house down?" I asked.

"My old life was over with that man anyway, so why not get rid of the house, too, and claim on the insurance? But now look what you've done. You ruined everything." Joni lunged for me, face full of vitriol, but Anxious growled a warning and she backed off.

"I don't get it," said Dad. "Why didn't you sell the house and business? You would most likely have got more than trying to claim on the insurance. What if they didn't pay out?"

"You stupid man!"

"Don't you call my Jack stupid," snarled Mum. "He's just a bit of a pilchard."

"Thanks, love." Dad grinned at Mum, then her words filtered in and he said, "I am not a pilchard."

"Explain yourself," demanded Liam, flexing a pec.

"The business isn't worth hardly anything. Dan made sure of that with his foul temper and even worse cooking. The house needed so many repairs we could never afford, and it was too much to handle. I wanted out. This was my chance. I had to take the opportunity once Carl was found dead. And just for the record, I truly had no idea who it was and hadn't even considered it was Dan's hunting buddy. She's to blame, not me." Joni jabbed a finger at Sue.

"But I didn't kill anyone," insisted Sue, clinging to Mickey.

"Yeah, she just wanted to give me something to do," said Mickey.

"I think we've heard enough." Sherry read Joni her rights, and once Liam had taken her away she turned to Sue and said, "You can come to the station when you're ready. I believe you, and I'm sure it will check out, but that was a very foolish thing you did."

"I know, and I'm so sorry."

With a happy wave, Sherry went to join Liam.

Nobody spoke or moved. We just watched Joni being put into a police car and driven away, then the peculiar detectives left, along with several other vehicles, while officers moved through the campsite then into the woods, presumably to secure the scene so it could be checked over properly now they knew the truth.

"Anyone fancy a cup of tea?" asked Mum.

Dad licked his lips. "Not half. I'm parched after all that running."

"I could go for one," said Mickey.

"Am I allowed?" asked Sue. "After what I did? I ruined your holiday. There was a dead man in your caravan. I got you all involved in this terrible mess, and because of me, Joni killed her husband and burned her house down."

"That's alright, love. We all do silly things now and then. And besides," said Mum, "you didn't make Joni do those things. It was her decision."

"And let's be honest," said Dad. "it's been an awesome few days. We got to have a lovely natter, went on nice walks, and it was a rocking murder mystery." Dad struck his best Elvis pose, wiggled his hips, and turned his lip up at the corner.

There was nothing I could do but laugh along with the others.

Bewildered by the turn of events, even though I'd figured out most of it after we'd found the shack, I became more focused on food once we got back to our pitch.

The beef stew smelled divine when I lifted the lid, so I put it back on a low heat once the tea was made, and settled on the floor of Vee with Anxious asleep inside on the bench seat.

The others sat on the blanket or chairs, lost to their own thoughts for a while, until Dad asked, "How did you figure it out, Son?"

"It was Sue's reaction when we saw the meat hanging. No offence, Sue, but I assumed you were rather squeamish, but you didn't seem that concerned. And when we were checking over the kiln there were clear signs of a disturbance around it. You have quite small feet, and I saw your footprints. It was a big oversight on your part, and if the police had found them before we disturbed the scene I'm sure they would have figured it out."

"I doubt it," said Mickey. "Most likely we'd have been long gone by then."

"That was it?" asked Sue. "My footprint?"

"And you made one other major mistake. Your hair was all over the motorbike. Anxious could smell you on it. That's why he was licking the seats. Not because of meat, but because it smelled like you. He likes you."

"Come on, mate, that can't be it," said Mickey. "How about Joni? Why did you suspect her?"

"Ah, that was different. Once I figured out about Sue, she was the obvious suspect. She clearly had issues with Dan, and with a murder on the premises it was the perfect opportunity to get rid of him. But it was because of the fire. It was obvious that was her."

"How so?" asked Sue.

"Because Joni made sure that both she and her son got out unharmed. We all saw the fire and how powerful it was, the damage it caused. She made certain Mike was somewhere in the house he could escape from easily, then she lit it and got him the moment it began. If he'd been upstairs he would have been killed. No, she sent him off on a pretence into a back room. She most likely had it set to light in the kitchen so it could be explained as a faulty appliance or a gas leak, and it would spread to the bar, then got her son straight away."

"That's a lot of guesswork, Max," said Mickey.

"No, it wasn't. It's the small signs that add up to big clues and help me figure things out. Joni knew exactly where the fire had started. How could she? And one other thing made me certain."

"What?" asked everyone, leaning forward.

"Joni lied about the hunting so she could avoid suspicion for the murder she didn't even commit. I saw both of them in the kitchen, and Dan was useless. She snatched a knife off him and cut up a large joint expertly. He didn't have a clue. Any hunter who goes out regularly would know how to butcher meat properly. When I told her about the shack, she said it was Dan, and she knew straight away it must have been Carl who was found."

"What a sneak," said Mickey.

"Yes. When she told me Dan hunted regularly, I was convinced she was lying. The rest just slotted into place. For a while, I thought she must have killed Carl, too, but she never wears trainers, unlike Sue, so the footprint at the shack couldn't have been hers. She also had a set of keys for the motorbike in her car. That made it obvious. She explained it by saying Dan had sets all over in case he lost them as he was forgetful, but the other possibility was that Joni used the motorbike as much as Dan, if not more."

"You are such a clever boy," said Mum, brimming with pride.

"So smart," agreed Dad with a wink.

"Thank you, but not really. It's more that I see things others overlook, and won't give up once I get started."

"Speaking of not giving up," said Dad, "I don't think I could give up on eating if you ever decide to serve dinner."

"Now you're talking," I grinned, then leaped up and sorted us out a fine meal.

The beef was incredibly soft, the carrots, onions, and thick stew an absolute delight. I felt as proud of this simple meal as anything else I'd done that day.

Although it was almost surreal to be sitting with Sue after what she'd done, I knew her heart was in the right place, although I would never be able to look at her in the same way again. She apologised repeatedly, and we all forgave her, but I wondered if that was really true as it was a terrible thing to have done.

But it was for love, and who doesn't do dumb things for the ones we love? I know I did.

Suddenly, I went cold, and my spoon clattered into my bowl.

"What's wrong?" asked Dad.

"I haven't called Min. She'll be livid I didn't tell her what's been going on. I thought she'd worry, so haven't called for days. When I do, she will not be a happy woman."

"Max, relax. Min knows you want her around. Once you explain, she won't be angry or anything," said Mum.

"I know that, but I promised to tell her if there was

another murder. I wanted to keep her away this time, but was going to call this morning to explain."

"There will always be a next time," said Dad.

"I think you might be right."

I called her later that evening once Mickey and Sue had got themselves ready, packed up, and driven to the police station. Mum and Dad sat enjoying an empty campsite, then once I'd explained to Min about what happened and she was nothing but happy everyone was alright, I returned to the pitch and had a pleasant evening.

My parents left the next morning, towing the pink caravan back to Sunny Parks. I wondered how Mike was doing, and what would happen to him without his parents around, but decided not to contact him as I wouldn't be his favourite person right now.

With Vee packed up, which took longer than usual because I had to sort out Mum's mess, I was done.

Almost.

There was one more thing left to do.

Chapter 19

I opened the gate then closed it behind me quietly, guilt washing over me for trespassing. The scent of the garden was almost overpowering now it was mid-morning, and I stopped for a moment to enjoy the results of the hard work that had gone into it.

I almost turned around and left, but knew my obsessive nature wouldn't allow it. I had to have answers and put this particular mystery to rest once and for all.

"I wondered how long it would take for you to return," said Constantine, a tinge of sadness in her voice as she smiled weakly then stood from the path where she was still murdering weeds.

"Once I begin something, I like to finish it. Sorry to intrude, and I know I should have called ahead, but didn't have your number."

"That's alright. I was expecting you anyway. In a way, it's a relief. I always wondered what happened, but now I know. What a fool I've been, but I guess I got what I deserved."

"Some of this I've figured out, but some of it I haven't. What I do know is that you were up in the clearing with Noel, but you said you'd never met him. That was a lie, wasn't it? You were in on this together, obviously, but not in the way the notes suggested."

"I would never hurt anyone! You don't think I…?"

"No, I don't." I fished out the earring back and handed it to Constantine. "Yours, I presume?"

She glanced down at the tiny piece of silver in her palm, then up at me, frowning. "Where did you find it? And how do you know it's mine?"

"Because you only have one earring. I thought that was strange, because people always have spares or just buy a new pair, but then it clicked. You only wear one because you lost the other the very last time you saw Noel, didn't you?"

"Yes, I did. I know it's silly, but it reminds me of him. I thought that maybe if I only wore the one earring he might return with it and surprise me. We'd laugh, then things would go back to how they were. Not that they were ever ideal, but I clung to it regardless. I'm just a daft, lonely woman who should know better, but you don't always get smarter as you get older. You mostly become more stubborn and meet fewer people. Sometimes it's hard." Constantine didn't attempt to hide the tears that fell freely. She kept her arms at her sides, clutching a trowel tightly, the path darkening for a moment before her tears evaporated with a faint sizzle.

"Let's go into the shade and we can talk," I suggested. "How about a cup of tea?"

"I'll got and make it. Max, I'm sorry I didn't tell you when you came before. It was mean-spirited and wrong. I was embarrassed, but that's no excuse."

"Constantine, there's no need to apologise. Let me clear one thing up first, just so you can relax a little. I'm not here to judge, and certainly not here to gloat about figuring this out. Whatever you did, it's nothing compared to the mess I made of my own life recently. Trust me, okay? It's all fine."

"You're a kind-hearted man, Max. Thank you."

While Constantine made tea, I settled in the shade while Anxious explored until he, too, needed to cool down so joined me.

Constantine arrived a few minutes later with two mugs of tea, and sat opposite me, her head lowered. Gradually, she raised her chin and our eyes met. Behind the tears, she was clearly a strong-willed woman, but something had gone wrong somewhere, and I think I knew what it was.

"You weren't the same after you lost your husband, were you?"

"No, I never quite recovered," she agreed, a wan smile morphing into a sharp laugh. "You must think I'm such a fool."

"I truly don't."

"I couldn't stay in our old home alone, and with no children I was bouncing around not knowing what to do. Do you have children, Max? They must be such a comfort."

"I don't, and I'm afraid I never will. Unless we adopt. It's complicated. I messed up my marriage and we divorced over a year ago. Now we're best friends, and I'm trying to win her back. I think I might, but we can't have children. We'll see what the future holds."

"I'm so sorry."

"Don't be. She's enough for me. More than I deserve. So you sold your old home?"

"Yes, once I found this place. A fresh start and all that. It's the silliest thing, really. One day I was walking through the woods and heard someone singing. I went to investigate and it was Noel. He was cooking sausages and singing happily. I startled him, then we got to chatting, and I ended up staying for the barbecue and a drink."

"He was alone?"

"Of course. Please believe me when I swear I never knew he had a wife."

"Come on, let's be honest. You mean you never discussed it, right?"

Constantine laughed, then admitted, "I didn't ask.

Max, we just clicked. Like two peas in a pod. For a while, I forgot about the old me and rediscovered a new, happy me. He made me happy. It was only for a weekend, and then he was gone. We didn't discuss the past, his other life, whatever that may be, and off he went."

"But he came back, didn't he?"

"He did. I never knew when. He would just turn up at the house. I can't even tell you how many times I walked up to the clearing hoping I'd see him, but he always surprised me here. A day here, a night there, sometimes a weekend. And then for the last few years we had a glorious fortnight. We laughed so much, were happy, but no, I never asked if he had a family, a wife, his job, any of it. I told him a little about my past, but not much, and I suppose it was like a dream. He was here, then he was gone. Then he simply never returned. I'd expected him this summer, but he never came, and I assumed that was the end of it. The mystery man was no more. It seems that's true, doesn't it? He's dead? Truly?"

"Yes, his wife, she—"

"I don't want to hear about it, Max. I'm sorry, but please let me at least have my memories of the time we spent together? Please?"

"Of course. I assumed that you had been together when we met you and I noticed the missing earring, but even before that, I think the flowers gave it away. He must have been drawn to you because of your love of gardening. He was a keen gardener too. You'd love the colour in his."

"I'm sure I would. We spent so many delightful days out here pottering about like we were an old married couple. I was beyond foolish, but I craved company and he was such a lovely man. What a silly fool I've been."

"There's nothing foolish about wanting company."

"No, but to steal another woman's husband is reprehensible. I knew deep down, but didn't want to face the reality."

"Now we get to the part I don't understand. The

notes. The scrap of paper behind the cupboard, and the one under the bed. What do they mean? Why were they written, let alone hidden like that?"

"They were a private joke, nothing more. You'll think it's silly, but the last time he stayed here, I spent the entire fortnight in the delightful campervan. When he wasn't there, I put the note under the bed."

"Ah, now it makes sense. It said you'd been stuck in the van for two weeks and didn't know if you'd get out alive. You spent two weeks with him and were fooling around?"

"Yes, a silly private joke. We used to pretend he'd held me captive. Just words, you understand? Nothing sinister. I thought it would make him smile when he found it, and I think deep down maybe I wanted someone else to find it. His wife. Is that ghastly?"

"It's not the best," I said diplomatically. "And the one that asked for help?"

"He always complained about the cupboard panel and said he'd fix it, but he never did. Another silly joke. Nothing more. Max, I'm deeply sorry for the anguish this has caused. You must have been so worried about what it all meant."

"It was very concerning, yes. I got the police involved as I told you, and couldn't stop thinking about it. But at least it's cleared up now."

"But that poor woman. What will she think?"

"His wife? She assumed it was grandchildren or friends messing around. And she always thought his van was in for a service for two weeks every year and he was working like normal."

"How did he manage to stay here for some of those nights?"

"He always went away now and then. She said he usually took a few days before and after the service. I guess that ties in with his stay?"

"It does. Max, don't think badly of me. Should I tell

his wife?"

"I can't offer advice on that. All I will say is that as far as she was concerned they had a happy marriage and she misses him terribly. What's the right thing to do is entirely up to you."

"Thank you for coming back. I feel so relieved. Like a weight has been lifted off my shoulders just by sharing this with you. But I apologise again for making you worry so much because of the notes."

"At least it's done with now. The main thing is, nobody was kidnapped. Noel didn't kill anyone, or hurt them."

"He just died. Here, then gone?"

"Yes, he just died."

With the tea drunk, and time getting on, Anxious and I said our goodbyes, then left Constantine to her garden.

Back in the clearing, with the breeze carrying the beautiful perfume our way, Anxious and I sat on the ground then lay back. As he shuffled in tight to my side, I stared up into the blue sky and finally felt at peace.

Sure, the world was a complicated place, and people struggled through as best they could. Sometimes we did the wrong thing, sometimes we did enough to make amends, but often we just winged it and hoped it would work out.

Maybe that was all we could ever do.

Maybe that was enough.

"Do you reckon we need to lighten our spirits, Anxious?" I asked, sitting bolt upright.

Anxious sat beside me, head cocked, ears primed for the good news.

"There's a comedy festival not too far away. I wasn't sure if we'd have time, but I guess we do now. It starts in a few days. Fancy it?"

Anxious barked an affirmative, so I checked on my phone, booked one adult, one under thirteen, and we were good to go.

"We need this. A few laughs, and absolutely no murders. It's only for a day, but we can camp there, so it'll be great fun."

The End

Except it isn't. Read on for another of Max's tasty one-pot wonders and a teaser about what to expect next. A Comedy of Terrors is the gang's seventh adventure, but will there be a mystery, or, eek, even a murder? Max's view might be different to ours, but let's find out, shall we?

But first, let's cook up a storm and finish off this latest instalment with a meal that will keep whoever does the washing up happy while you order the next book.

Recipe

British Beef Stew (because you can't beat it!)

There are a million ways to cook an awesome beef stew. Good stock, booze if you fancy, time, and a decent cut of beef are always a good start. Mushrooms, tomato puree, bay leaves, parsnips, swede, butter beans, or even some strong cheddar stirred in at the end will all work.

This one is a family favourite and features Marmite. You can't get more British. Even the weird Marmite haters (which is what my son calls me, but he is wrong!) will love it, but for those deprived of this controversial condiment in their pantry add some Worcestershire, Vegemite, or miso paste instead.

Ingredients

- Vegetable oil - 2-3 tbsp
- Beef - something that will take slow cooking and just get more delightful - shin, braising steak or similar, diced into large chunks - around a kilo (2lb)
- An onion - finely sliced
- Two garlic cloves - crushed
- Two sticks of celery - chopped
- Baby carrots - 500g (1lb) trimmed, washed, and left whole
- Plain flour - 2 tbsp
- Beef stock (500ml / 1pt)
- Stout / dark beer or more stock - 350ml (2/3 pt)
- Wholegrain mustard - 1 tbsp
- Marmite - 2 tsp
- Caster sugar - 2 tsp
- Thyme - a few sprigs

- Salt and freshly ground black pepper to taste

Method

- In your lovely cast-iron Dutch oven, casserole, or similarly big pan, heat half the oil on a medium high heat. Now brown the beef in batches so as not to overcrowd the pot. Add more oil as needed and put each batch of lovely golden meat to one side.
- Once all the meat is caramelised, turn the heat down and sauté the onion for ten minutes or so to soften gently. Scrape and stir any delicious beefy bits from the bottom of the pan into the onions. Once translucent, you can add the garlic, celery, and carrots. Give it all a good stir around until everything's glossy.
- Add the beef back to the pan and stir in the flour.
- Pour over your liquid of choice and stir in the mustard, Marmite, sugar, and thyme, along with a pinch of salt and a grinding of pepper.
- Bring to the boil, then turn down the heat, cover, and let it blip away slowly for two and a half hours until the beef is soft, and the stew is thickened. You'll need to keep an eye on it for the last half an hour or so to make sure it doesn't catch on the bottom of the pan. Adjust the seasoning before serving.

Enjoy with mash, crusty bread, or under a pastry top. Alternatively, go for all three, but be sure to loosen your belt! That's not quite one-pot cooking either, but they are certainly options. Of course dumplings would be authentic, but in these parts simply not worth the hassle—bread's lovely enough, eh?

From the Author

Grisly or what!? Ugh. Makes me shudder.

Thanks so much for reading, and I would like to take this opportunity to let you know that the kind comments, reviews, and continued sales for this series have been very heartening.

So, you continue to read, and I'll continue to write. Deal? Great!

Now, let's get down to what's really on all our minds.

What's next for Max and Anxious? Time to find out…

Continue Max's Campervan Case Files in A Comedy of Terrors. It's going to be awesome. I can guarantee you several things: a murder, a mystery, and there might even be a few laughs along the way. There will also definitely be biscuits for Anxious, and some stunning one-pot meals made by Max. I hope that you've tried some of the recipes. If not, then why not grab your biggest pot and give one a go? You can't go far wrong with beef stew, and it's perfect for one-pot cooking.

Let's get to it…

Be sure to stay updated about new releases and fan sales. You'll hear about them first. No spam, just book updates at www.authortylerrhodes.com.

You can also follow me on Amazon www.amazon.com/stores/author/B0BN6T2VQ5.

Connect with me on Facebook www.facebook.com/authortylerrhodes/

Printed in Dunstable, United Kingdom